A Night at the Y

a collection of short stories by

Robert Garner McBrearty

*To Karen and Steve,
in friendship and appreciation,
Robert Garner McBrearty*

1999
JOHN DANIEL & COMPANY
SANTA BARBARA, CALIFORNIA

Published by John Daniel & Company
A division of Daniel and Daniel, Publishers, Inc.
Post Office Box 21922
Santa Barbara, CA 93121

LIBRARY OF CONGRESS CATALOGING-IN-PUBLICATION DATA
McBrearty, Robert.
    A night at the Y / by Robert McBrearty.
    ISBN 1-880284-36-7 (alk. paper)
    1. Southwestern States—Social life and customs—Fiction.   2. West
(U.S.)—Social life and customs—Fiction.   I. Title.
PS3563.C33358N54   1999
813'.54—dc21   99-12912
                                                            CIP

A Night at the Y

In memory of my loving mother,

Virginia Garner McBrearty,

to all my wonderful family,

to my treasures, Zane and Ian,

to my beloved Mary Ellen,

and with a special thanks

to my old friend and teacher

Leonard Wallace Robinson

Contents

GRATEFUL ACKNOWLEDGEMENT is made to the following publications in which some of these stories were first published: *The Missouri Review*: "A Night at the Y," "Back in Town"; *Mississippi Review*: "The Dishwasher," "The Hellraiser"; *New England Review*: "First Day"; *Kansas Quarterly*: "Improvising"; *Confrontation*: "The Unfolding"; *Crescent Review*: "The Pearl Diver"; *Sycamore Review*: "Soft Song of the Sometimes Sane"; *Shankpainter*: "My Life As a Judo Master"; *Peregrine*: "The Yellow House"; *Zone 3*: "The Things I Don't Know About."

"The Dishwasher" was reprinted in *The Pushcart Prize: Best of the Small Presses*; "The Hellraiser" was reprinted in *Special Report*.

A Night at the Y

FINISHED WITH HIS DAY JOB, Ralph stops back at his apartment just long enough to change clothes and kiss his wife and baby goodbye before rushing off to his night shift at the Y. He stands behind the front desk, with his left hand picking up phones and with his right dispensing towels and locker keys. With a harried grin, caffeine-inspired energy, and the sinking realization that there is baby spit-up on his blue sweater, he greets the incoming members who are frantic to run, swim, lift, jiggle, jazz, and whirlpool away the jangled nerves of a long day in this fast-paced city just east of the Rocky Mountains. As the members burst through the front doors, stomp snow from their boots, and charge the desk with lowered heads and hunched shoulders, they remind him of truculent bulls, and he is transported by a memory of a day in a mountain town in Mexico twenty years before.

The bulls are poised in the cattle truck, ready for the run. Ralph, twenty-one years old then, full of wild hope and amoebic parasites, dagger-thin and crazed from dysentery and ingestions of medicinal tequila, has taken refuge on the steps of El Patio Café.

Nine bulls come down the ramp—motley, scraggly, apathetic bulls to be sure. No monsters of Pamplona in this September fiesta. They clomp into the roped-off square and the crowd lets out a collective half-gasp, half-giggle as it huddles against the barriers and gathers on the steps of the café. Young men prance in the cobblestone streets, whistling and jeering. The bulls come to a standstill, snort, wheeze, roll anxious eyes about. Perhaps in the backs of their dim brains flickers the uneasy suspicion that this bacchanal can only finish with them on the wrong end of a public barbecue.

These humble, pastoral beasts see no cause for confrontation. They show no inclination to trample, hook with their horns or spew foam. They'd like to laugh this off; couldn't it all be resolved peacefully? They stomp on the cobblestones, leaning their heads together, discussing their strategy as their breath rises in white puffs on this crisp, blue Sunday afternoon in late September. They try to back up the ramp into the truck, but four exasperated rancheros swing cowboy hats at their rumps; disconsolately, the bulls come forward into the sunny but bracing afternoon, and the crowd releases another excited cry.

In his memory, Ralph sees himself backing up as high as he can on the café steps, wending his way behind children and serape-wrapped women. But the other young men, so boldly challenging the bulls, seem to beckon to him: Come down! Run with the bulls! And briefly he yearns to encounter his fate, to die on those dusty cobblestone streets with a horn in his chest, blood in his boots, a wine flask tipped to his lips, while his fingers rise and twitch gracefully, keeping time with the mariachi music as he fades...on brave marvelous soul!

The rank odor of sweat and soggy towels and leather basketballs wafts over the desk, and from the gym comes the reverberation of bouncing balls and the trill of a referee's whistle. Ralph's memory of the fiesta momentarily slips away and he finds himself back at the Y desk, in the present, though he wonders, given the vast and inexplicable discoveries of modern physics, just exactly what is the present. His uncertainty about the nature of time makes him suddenly aware that he will never be able to explain modern physics to his son, or even cogently describe the inner workings of a telephone. Thinking of his inadequacies as a father makes his heart flutter as he continues handing out towels and keys.

His rush-hour helper, Maggie Vivigino, the twenty-two-year-old, green-eyed olive-skinned weight room trainer, joins him

behind the counter. Her taut body ripples beneath her purple leo-
tard, and Ralph imagines she would have made a wonderful com-
panion for his former self when he was cringing on the steps of El
Patio Café. But Maggie, he suspects, considers him a loser, working
at the Y at his age, though she kindly tries to conceal the feeling.

The evening rush speeds up. The Y members, punchy and
frayed from another hectic workday, will brook no delay, resent
showing their membership cards.

"Don't you know who I am by now?"

"I want a good locker tonight! Last time you stuck me in a drafty
corner."

"When are you people going to get your act together?"

Meanwhile the phone lines are ringing urgently, the red buttons
pulsating; the callers are desperate with weighty questions. Ralph
stabs at buttons, puts people on hold, accidentally disconnects a
few.

"Where is my son's soccer game tomorrow?" a caller inquires.
"He lost his schedule and I don't have the coach's number."

"How do I sign up for the karate class?"

"Where is the director? I want to speak to the director."

"Have you seen a woman in a green bikini?"

"The Y? I wanted Pete's Pool Hall. How long have you had this
number?"

"Who's in charge there? I want to speak to the director!"

"If you see a woman in a green bikini, tell her I want to meet
her."

"Are you sure this is the Y?"

"If I sign up for the karate class, do I need to know how to kick
beforehand?"

"Listen, this is serious. I've got to find out about my kid's soccer
game...."

Unfortunately, Ralph has little information to dispense. His job
is to answer calls and forward them to the appropriate offices. But
it is Friday evening and the director and administrators have fled
the building.

"Would you mind if I put you on hold?" Ralph says for the hun-
dredth time.

"Yes, I would mind. I've been on hold twice already. Can't you just tell me where my son's damn soccer game is tomorrow?" By this time, the soccer man's voice has turned thick, hoarse and boozy.

"I'm sorry. I don't have the schedule here. I just answer the phones and forward them to the program desk."

"Then let me have the program desk."

"I'm afraid they're closed. They don't open again until nine in the morning."

"But the game is at eight! You people are screwed up, you hear me? Screwed up!"

"Ralph! Help!" Maggie screams from her station behind the desk. Ralph turns from the phone to see a fresh wave of incoming customers.

"I'm afraid I'm going to have to put you on hold, sir. I'll find out what I can."

"Don't you put me—"

He joins the fray and confronts a woman who snarls, "This is the longest I've ever had to wait. Can't you make your calls on your own time?"

A man flings his key back onto the desk. "This is a boy's locker," he hisses in righteous rage.

A tall, bearded man takes a towel from Ralph's trembling hand and inquires cheerfully, "Are we having fun yet?"

Right in front of the customers, Maggie puts her hands to her face and screams, as she screams nearly every day at this time, "I'm quitting! I'm quitting!"

The members meet this pronouncement with a stony indifference, and she continues snatching cards from their hands and hurling their locker keys and towels at them.

Then suddenly the wave dissipates; the customers disappear into the locker rooms and quiet settles over the front desk as another rush hour at the Y comes to a close. Maggie looks at Ralph with a bright mist in her eyes. "This is what I get for not finishing college. I'll always work at crappy jobs."

He takes her aside, draws her back to the tall metal equipment lockers, thinks of holding her steely biceps, but doesn't. He assures her she can still go back and finish college, though inside a subversive voice whispers: Of course you can finish college like I did and still work at crappy jobs.

As night deepens, only a few people straggle in from the snow. The calls, too, have slackened, though the soccer man keeps phoning, sounding drunker and more abusive each time he calls. Maggie has returned to the weight room to Stairmaster away her blues; her sinewy legs provide inspiration to all the panting after-hours jocks.

Ralph calls his wife and she groans with fatigue. Their six-month-old boy has been crying for hours.

"What did the doctor say?"

"It's probably just teething."

"How long do you think it will last?"

"About ten more years." She sniffles, "I think I'm losing it."

"Courage, love," he whispers, "courage."

He slips away from the quiet desk to take the dirty towels to the laundry room, and his heart twists as the sweet strains of Joni Mitchell drift from the overhead speakers:

I was a free man in Paris
I felt unfettered and alive....

Alive and unfettered indeed, Ralph, on that day twenty years ago, huddles on the café steps as the bulls make rings around the square and feign charges at the young men. The bold ones rush among the bulls, slap rumps and pull horns, and when the bulls are inspired enough to give chase, the young men dive for cover at the last moment.

Ralph remains on his perch, cautiously watching the action. He detects about him, in subtle glances and stiffened shoulders, the faint signs of disgust: Oh, cowardly American, go down with the other young men and do battle with these ferocious bulls!

Out of nowhere, a boy of about four has wandered into the middle of the street in front of the café. Too late, the crowd on the café steps spots him. In the same moment a bull, ten yards away, lowers its horns and charges.

The crowd is paralyzed, deathly still, as if by holding its breath it can make the bull turn aside. Then its silence gives way to a panicked roar. Ralph is not certain, but later he thinks that he felt a push on his back—a palpable, yet unearthly touch. Barely conscious of what he is doing he rushes through the crowd—a fish gliding past boulders that give way to him—and leaps off the steps. Too late to sweep the boy aside, he runs directly in front of the bull. He feels a bone-jarring impact in his side; his shoes seem stuck to the pavement while the rest of his body flies upwards. He is totally breathless, yet at the same time trying to puke. He's vaguely aware of sailing beneath a blue sky before he loses consciousness.

As he awakens, a wooden ceiling fan is twirling slowly overhead. His eyes flicker open and shut, open and shut. The examining table is hard, and the scent of alcohol is familiar and comforting. The doctor and his nurse are marvelously efficient and reassuring as they smile down on him and tape his ribs. The young doctor is dashing in his street clothes; called away from the fiesta, he smells of beer and his eyes glitter. The nurse wears a low-cut flowery dress, and she leans over him and caresses his brow with a moist palm.

"How are you feeling now, my hero friend?" the doctor says, with only a slightly Spanish accent.

Ralph blinks. "Is the boy okay?"

The doctor and his nurse grin at one another, and their eyes shine. "The boy is fantastic," the doctor says. "And you will be okay. It's the bull we are worried about now."

The doctor and his nurse fall against each other in a paroxysm of laughter and then topple lightly onto Ralph, who puts his arms around their quaking backs.

"Kay wise guy, where's the soccer game? Tell me where my son's soccer game is. I'm not dropping this."

"Look, I've done everything I can. I even tried to call the program director at home, but there was no answer. I don't know what else I can do."

"That won't do, my friend. That won't do. I only see my kid every fourth weekend. You're not screwing this up for him. Somebody knows. Somebody there knows." His voice rises, takes on a chanting quality: "Somebody knows, somebody there knows, somebody knows...."

"Look, I'm really sorry. But I've got to get off now."

"Don't you cut me off, you son of a bitch. Don't you—"

Ralph stares at the phone, but it doesn't ring again. He almost regrets it because there is a sadness at the Y now as the hour grows late. Most of the members and all the other attendants have come and gone, and there are no distractions from his worries. He wonders if his family will make it in this new part of the country they have moved to. Will he find a better job? Will his son be happy growing up here, in this town hard-pressed against the Rockies? Will his wife's health, already fragile, hold through the fitful nights as they get up again and again to comfort the baby?

Out of the dark comes a family, a father, a mother, and a boy of about four. As they come through the front doors they pause, half inside and half out. Behind them, the night pours snow; a gust of frigid air rushes all the way to Ralph at the front desk. They hesitate in the doorway. Then the man gives the boy a gentle nudge, and they all come forward anxiously toward the desk.

The man, about Ralph's age, is short, thick, bearded, with a burly chest and wide hunched shoulders; he looks as if he has seen a lot of rough weather, done a lot of hard labor, yet there is something weak about him. His smile is tremulous. The woman is Hispanic, with dark somber eyes. When they reach the desk, the man keeps his family huddled close, one hand resting on the boy's black hair, the other holding his wife's elbow through her old flannel coat. In a quavering Texas accent, his voice coming out high at first before it finds its range, he says, "Hi. Think you can rent us a room?" He shrugs apologetically. "We can't pay motel prices."

The one word Ralph doesn't want to say to the worn-out looking family is no, but this is what he must tell them.

"I'm sorry, but I'm afraid we don't rent overnight rooms here. We're mainly a gym. The Y in Denver rents some rooms."

The man's shoulders slump another notch. The woman's eyes explore Ralph's face, searching for lies. "Damn. We came through there an hour ago," the man says mournfully. "We're headed for Seattle...from Houston," he adds, as if that explains their plight. He shakes his head and mutters, almost as if repeating a mantra, "Got good jobs in Seattle. Houston ain't nothing but a bust." The woman nods grimly, agreeing with him about Houston. Ralph wonders if she believes in the good jobs ahead.

Ralph sees that they are all dead tired. The man and woman glance sidelong at one another, calculating the time back to Denver, this late at night, in the bad weather, the lost time on their journey; the decision is coming down against it.

He is tempted to offer them lodging in his cramped little apartment for the night. But what would his wife say? Too dangerous to bring strangers in. Even though she is kind-hearted, her fears for their son would make her say no. He knows he is only using her as an excuse, though. Even if he lived alone he wouldn't offer, wouldn't want to be drawn into their troubles. But the dark, round, staring eyes of the little boy remind him of what his own family might come to under different circumstances, adrift in a strange city, no money for a motel.

"There is a hostel by the campus," he says slowly.

The man blinks. "A hostel?"

"It's kind of like a dorm, but you don't have to be students. It's only a few dollars to stay there."

The man glances at his wife, still clutching her elbow. She looks at him, and then down at her son. She puts her hand on the boy's head and draws him tighter against her leg. She angles her thin face away from the man and her jaw stiffens, a shift which seems to freeze the man. There is something about the word hostel, Ralph sees, which has stopped her, become a stumbling block.

The man sighs and turns back to Ralph. "We'll go on and look for a motel, I guess. You know anything cheap? It don't have to be nothing fancy."

"I haven't lived here too long myself, but we can look through the Yellow Pages. Most things are kind of expensive in this town, though."

As he reaches under the desk for a phone book, a sheet of pink, lined paper flutters out; he glances idly at it for a moment, and then stares in amazement at the columns of writing. He slips the sheet of paper under his sweater into the top pocket of his shirt and pats it to secure its position, as if the paper is some treasure of great worth.

The man stands at the front desk, thumbing through the Yellow Pages and making his calls from the desk phone. He stumbles over his questions, his brow furrowing as if he can't quite figure out what people are telling him. With each call, his voice quavers more; sweat springs out on his forehead and his blunt stubby finger makes mistakes dialing. Ralph eases the phone away from him and makes a few calls himself, but it is a football weekend and the motels are either full or too expensive.

Because he can't bring himself to offer his apartment, he says instead, knowing the inadequacy of the offer, "May I buy you all a cup of coffee? And a hot chocolate for your son?"

The man, who has gone back to calling himself, holds the phone to his chest, momentarily stunned by the offer. The boy's eyes brighten as he looks over at the coffee machine against the wall. The woman moves away from the man's side. As if it's a way of saying yes, she wraps her arms around herself, gives an exaggerated, friendly sort of shiver, and says, "It's cold here."

Ralph makes change in the register and goes around the desk into the lobby. The boy follows him to the machine. He takes hold of Ralph's pant leg and stares silently as the cup drops down and fills. The woman wanders over to the green vinyl chairs, set in a circle around a worn coffee table, and sits down. She lifts a magazine and crosses one slim leg over the other, frowning at the no smoking sign on the wall. Ralph distributes the coffees and hot chocolate. As the few remaining members drift out from the locker rooms, the woman, unlit cigarette in mouth, stares at them with narrowed eyes. The boy follows Ralph as he makes a quick tour of the offices in back, making sure doors and windows are locked. The boy slips his hand into Ralph's and as he holds the tiny, cool little hand, he wishes he could do some finer thing.

With his ribs taped tightly, Ralph rises stiffly from the examining table. The doctor and nurse help him back into his shirt, and the nurse kisses him on the cheek and ushers him into the waiting room where a small entourage rises and cheers him as he wobbles forward. They offer to see him home, but what he really wants is tequila, he tells them. His request is greeted with a chorus of approval and he is taken up by his new friends and escorted to a cantina near the square, where he drinks icy Tecate beer and shots of José Cuervo, and his newfound best friends embrace him again and again.

Later, he will dimly recall making fervid offers to take his friends to a ranch in Montana where they would live off the land and practice medieval chivalry. "You will need English lessons, Juan," he recalls himself saying to one particularly affectionate but incoherent man who kept putting him in headlocks and lowering his nose to the bar.

A bloody sunset glows over the ancient mountain town as he stumbles out the swinging cantina doors; he is on the march again with his entourage, this time slipping through the barricades back into the square where the bulls, at last thoroughly pissed off, have gone into higher gear and are managing to hook a few overconfident young campesinos in the seats of their jeans.

For what seems like hours then, but what must have been, in reality, only a few glorious minutes, he experiences what feels like saintliness. The bulls cannot hurt him. They charge at him and he stands motionless; at the last moment, he gives a sweep of his hands and sends them veering away. When he sees anyone in trouble, a bull moving in, he glides over and with a light touch on the rump turns the bull aside. The townsfolk scream his glory, a great roar rising from behind the barricades. They scream the only name they know for him: *"Gringo! El Gringo!"* Sombreros fly his way, coins, roses; a beer can bounces off the side of his head.

But back at the Y, saintliness is in short supply. The man is running out of motels to call and it is nearing midnight. The Y will close in ten minutes. Only a diehard weightlifter or two remain somewhere in the dank bowels of the building.

It is time for the nightly closing announcement, which Ralph amends from night to night. Over the intercom system, his voice echoes back at him, "Another night at the Y is fast drawing to a close. Prepare to go forth, repaired of body, mind, and spirit...."

The man pauses with his finger on the Yellow Pages and gives him a pained smile. Turning, the man signals to his wife, who rises

wearily from her chair and joins him. The boy, who has been staring mesmerized through the plate glass doors at the silent blue
swimming pool, comes over and leans his sleepy head against his
mother's legs. The man closes the phone book and says to his family, "Looks like we'll rest up in the truck tonight." His voice is a dry
whisper, "We can run the engine enough to keep warm."

The woman nods, her lips forming a tight line, and Ralph notes
that she is not blaming the man, or trying to make him feel worse,
which somehow makes him feel sorrier for them. He thinks again
of inviting them to his home for the night, but is silent. The boy
presses himself tighter against his mother's legs. The man shuts his
eyes for a long moment, rubbing the back of his neck and swinging
his head like a tired old bull. When he opens his eyes and stares
across the front desk at Ralph, he looks amazed to discover himself
here, at this moment in time. Slowly, he sticks his hand out across
the counter and Ralph grasps it. The man's hand is dry and rough.
He shakes without force. "Thank you, sir. You were real helpful.
We thank you."

"I wish I could help, but—"

"We'll be okay." The woman's blunt tone silences him. She
kneels, pulls her son's hood up and ties the drawstring. Though he
is old enough to walk alone, she cradles him and hoists him to her
chest.

Ralph comes around the desk and follows them toward the
front door. They are halfway through the lobby when a tall shape
appears on the other side of the glass doors; a man, clutching his
jacket to guard his neck from the cold, lurches in from the snowy
night, followed by a stream of frigid air. He shivers, stamps snow
from his shoes, and glares wild-eyed at Ralph and the little family.
He charges forward.

Ralph moves in front of the family. "May I help you?"

"You work here? You're the one I've been talking to?" His head
bobs on a long neck. He glowers. His face is flushed, and his breath
reeks of whiskey.

The family shrinks back behind Ralph as the stranger points his
car keys at Ralph's chest. "I drove all the way through the fucking
snow and ice, pal, to personally chew out your ass, and I'd better

get some straight answers this time. Where is my son's soccer game? Where, dammit?"

Ralph stares at the man. Then he reaches under his sweater and whips out a pink sheet of paper. "Which team?"

"What's that?" The man blinks. "The...Rockets. Yeah, the Rockets." He squints at the schedule Ralph is holding.

"El Centro Elementary. Folsom Street. Eight A.M."

The man rocks back on his heels as if someone had struck him, then tips forward, pressing the points of his keys to Ralph's chest. The astonishment in his face turns to rage, "Why did you make me go through hell to—"

"Easy," Ralph says. "Easy," and he takes the man by the arms. Gently and gracefully Ralph walks, almost waltzes him the few steps to the coffee table. He pushes the man down in a chair, and takes his car keys. "I'll call you a cab."

The man tries to rise, but Ralph puts a hand on his chest. The calmness of his own voice startles him. "It's that or I can call the police."

The man stares up at him drunkenly. He stiffens as if to fight, and then collapses. He sinks back in the chair and with a defeated expression he looks about the lobby for someone to make his case to; finally, his eyes light on the wall photos of the Y board members, and to their smiling, broad faces he protests, "What a fucked up place this is." But he stays put, shivering, letting out disgruntled sighs and groans as a puddle of melted snow forms around his shoes.

Meanwhile, Ralph sees that the family has slipped away. He rushes into the night and sees them trudging across the parking lot in the snow, the boy over his mother's shoulder. "Hey!" he calls, running after them. "Wait!" They glance back, but hurry on for their truck.

Catching up with them, lightly touching the man's elbow, he talks quickly, getting the offer out before he can stop himself. "You can spend the night with us if you like. It's not much. We'll have to put out sleeping bags on the floor. And we have a baby who's been crying a lot. But it's warm. You can stretch out. Have a shower in the morning. Breakfast...."

The man's eyes widen and he looks in consternation from Ralph to his wife. She holds her boy tighter to her breasts and Ralph speaks to her now. "It's all right. Really. It's no problem. I want you to stay with us."

Her face hardens, and for a scary moment he thinks she is going to tell him to shove his offer; then, in an instant, her face softens and he sees something more frightening: he believes she is going to cry. She gives his hand a light squeeze, and nods faintly.

"Okay," Ralph says. "Okay. Great."

His shoulders relax and drop, his chest expands; an adrenalin-like thrill rushes through him. Turning, he lifts his face to the wet white shower of snow and starts back for the Y. The family follows close behind him, as if they are afraid to lose him.

And twenty years in the past (though, given the vast and inexplicable discoveries of modern physics, who can say just what the past is) he is seized by two policemen. One of them screams in his face, "Out of the street, *cabrón*! You want to get killed?"

They give him the bum's rush out of the square. Then he is weaving home through the cobblestone streets, followed by his loyal entourage and a ragged mariachi band…weaving his way home through the last bloody rays of the sunset, weaving below the flowered balconies, a beautiful woman waving from a window…the bugles serenading a young man home as he takes a glorious walk toward the future, toward a long wintry night at the Y.

The Hellraiser

IT'S NEW YEAR'S EVE, and I'm raising hell. I've driven my truck into town and tried to call the boys together. But each year there's more guys settling down, getting married, dulling out, and this year I'm down to Leon and his tag-along little brother, Sam.

We're at a topless bar, sitting a few feet from the stage where these not-too-gorgeous girls are shaking their stuff with a certain enthusiasm, if not beauty. A disc jockey plays hard-edged jungle rock and strobe lights flash. There's red and silver streamers hanging from the ceiling to give the bar a holiday spirit, but the crowd's small and quiet and seems more interested in the popcorn than in the girls.

Old Leon, who used to be crazy, always ready for fun, keeps checking his watch and saying we ought to go. He told his wife, Beth, that we'd be back after one drink out, to spend New Year's Eve with her and their kid. Leon's my best old buddy, though he's not much of a hellraiser anymore. He's starting to get as dulled out as everybody else. When I come into town now, I feel like he doesn't even really want me here. Or he partly does, but he partly doesn't, too. It's too hard for him to fit me in. He needs to have everything planned out, like he's always running on a time clock. It drives me crazy.

A dancer bends over with her legs spread and grabs her ankles.

She lowers her head and stares at us upside down from between her legs.

"Look at that flexibility," I say, but the boys don't seem very impressed. "Go baby!" I encourage her. I grab one of the noisemakers that the waitresses have passed out and blow it. "This is fun," I say.

"I've really got to get going," Leon says.

"Yeah, the smoke is destroying my sinuses," Sam says.

He keeps snorting nose spray every few minutes. For a guy who's only twenty, ten years younger than me and Leon, he sure is acting dulled out. "The hell with your nose," I say. "Let's have some real fun."

Leon and Sam are both short, well-built guys. In fact, none of us is over five foot seven. "Look," I say, "let's go up on stage and tell people we're a short men's wrestling team and challenge anyone to come up and wrestle with us. We'll find out who the real men are."

I start standing up and Leon grabs me by the wrist and pleads, "C'mon now, Rhino." That's one of my old nicknames. The Rhino. I've sort of let that one slide. Mostly now, people call me Scooter.

I sit back down. Blow my noisemaker. Leon checks his watch again. It's getting harder and harder to raise hell these days.

All afternoon as I was driving in from Irving, I was getting in a crazy mood, wearing my hat with the deer antlers, honking my horn at any girls I passed on the highway. Sometimes the girls would laugh and wave. It seemed to take the chill out of the day. For a while, I was thinking maybe I'd meet a girl at a roadside park, at a gas station, the Stuckey's, the Colonel's Kentucky Fried, you never know. But mostly it just seemed like the cows were watching me, standing behind the barbed wire fences, wondering if they were going to get rained on. Cows always look depressed and lonely and like they're hoping you can do them a favor. I grew up in the country. I hate the country.

When I got to San Antone, that seemed pretty bad, too, with all the freeways. God, freeways are ugly. Leon's neighborhood is boring, with the nice, one-story pink brick houses with white shutters. There seems to be exactly three trees in every front yard. Everybody looks thirty here, except the kids, who ride around on bicycles with tall, red flags on the back so that people will see them and not run them over. Their dads thought of the flags. I don't think I'd want a kid and have to worry about that kind of stuff. I drove into Leon's driveway honking my horn. Some guy was next door washing his car, and he looked at me, noticing my deer antler hat. "How you doing there, pistol?" I called, wanting to liven up his evening a little.

"Okay," he said, but he sounded kind of dulled out.

Beth opened the door and said, "You're here." It could have been meant a lot of ways. Leon was sitting on the couch with his four-year-old, Ron. They were watching a show about animals. Ron threw a plastic astronaut at me and said, "You're Darth Vader."

I had to get Leon out of the house for a while. I just couldn't let him sit home and watch TV on New Year's Eve. I felt like I owed him that much.

Now this Chicana woman is dancing. She's a big sort of woman. Big everything. I like big, tough-bellied women. And that face ain't gonna win no awards. Crooked nose, mean eyes, kinky black hair, teeth that maybe somebody took a pliers to. But it all comes together into something I like. She's got soul. I can picture her with a broken bottle taking on a gang of drunken sailors. She leaves them whimpering. She dances without much style, but closes her eyes like she can feel herself in the arms of a lover.

"I've really got to go, Scooter. I'm late already," Leon says. "Beth's just sitting at home getting mad. I know."

"You don't know how to have fun anymore, Leon. If you can't have a drink with your old buddy on New Year's Eve, then I give up. You might as well go to bed and just stay there."

"I'm having fun," Leon says, but he doesn't sound like it.

"And you, all you worry about is your nose," I say to Sam. "Hell, when I was twenty...."

The song finishes and the dancer looks over at the guy who's sitting behind the window playing the records. She puts an arm over her bare breasts. Then the music starts again, a really fast one. She's got her eyes open now, and she's laughing, throwing her head around. Reaching her arms out to the crowd like she's inviting us up on the stage, she shouts, "C'mon you deadbeats. Somebody clap!" I blow my noisemaker. Somewhere over in the corner another guy gives a halfhearted clap. She's right. Everybody's acting like a deadbeat. I bet there's some real buffaloes in here, too, if they'd just loosen up. Cowboys wanting to ride out with some tough hell-for-leather woman. They just need someone to shake them into life, to help them see the possibilities. And it looks like it's going to a have to be me who does it.

"Watch this," I say to the boys. "I'll show you fun." And with a hop, like springing over a fence, I'm up on the stage with her. I dance, wiggling my rear, sticking my chest out.

"Whoo-oo," she shouts. "A live one."

"Whoo-oo," I hoot. I try to pull my sweater off, but it gets stuck, covering my eyes. I'm blinded. The dancer's got me by the shoulders, and she's spinning me around like a top. I hear the whole bar laughing, blowing their noisemakers, clapping. People are having some real fun now, coming alive. Everybody's got a mission in life. Sometimes it wears heavy. She lets go of me and I fumble out of my sweater and toss it to Leon. I'm unbuttoning my shirt, and the dancer's grinding away. I can't hear over the music, but she's mouthing the words, "Go go go."

I shout, "Go go go."

The song cuts off suddenly, and I can hear that she's saying, "No no no."

"No?"

"Don't take your clothes off. Go sit down, buddy. You've had enough fun."

To a thunderous applause, with a few boos mixed in, popcorn flying everywhere, I jump off the stage and sit back down with the boys. They look sheepish, shoulders sort of hunkered over, glancing around sidelong.

"Well, I guess you enjoyed yourself," Leon says.

"Well, hell yes, I did."

Across the bar, I see a cute little silver-haired waitress. I signal her over so that I can order some more drinks. Up close, I realize she's old. Her face is dried out and wrinkled. Her blue shadowed eyes and blood red lipstick make her look like she's wearing a mask. But she looks like she's still holding on to a dream that she's good-looking, that men still want her; that dream is good for her, all that keeps her going.

"What's it going to be, honey?" she asks.

"Nothing," Leon says. "Sorry. No thanks. We have to get going. I have a commitment."

"I have a commitment, too," I say. I stand up and put my arm around the waitress. With one hand she balances her drink tray that's loaded with empties, and slips her free arm around my waist. I hold her tight. "This is my life," I say. "This is what I live for."

Leon and Sam look at me like I've gone crazy. The waitress squeezes me. "It's okay, sugar, sure you do."

But you can only hold an aging waitress for so long. I feel defeated by something I can't name. "Never mind, honey. I guess we're going."

Beth and the kid are sitting on the couch, sort of dulled out, looking like they've dozed and woken, dozed and woken. They're watching a hospital show. Some doctors and nurses are wearing masks and making jokes while they take out some sorry guy's gall bladder. Beth is sipping a green drink that makes her lips pucker.

"Well, hey hey, Happy New Year, honey," Leon says.

She gives us a withering look, stands up and disappears into the hallway.

"Oh great," Leon says to the people in the TV.

"Well, I guess we were late," I say.

Old Ron's got that plastic astronaut in his hand again, and damn if he doesn't chunk it at me.

"How come you didn't play with me tonight, Daddy, stupid idiot?"

"I'll play," Leon says. "Hey, I'll play." He scoops Ron off the couch and runs around the room with him, supporting him underneath the belly and legs, making a torpedo or a bird out of Ron's body. "Superboy. Look at Superboy fly."

Ron giggles. "Superman, Daddy." They swoop into the hallway, going after Beth.

"How about a drink?" I ask Sam.

"I've got to breathe some steam first."

"Christ, are you sick or what?"

"I've been sick for three months."

I find a bottle of tequila in the liquor cabinet over the kitchen sink. Sam puts a pot of water on the stove to boil. He bends over it with a towel draped over his head and makes snorting sounds like a Zambezi hippo.

I carry my drink into the empty den and look at the TV. A stretcher with a screaming patient strapped in is rolling down a steep hill. In San Francisco maybe. I turn the TV off.

Leon comes back into the room carrying Ron in one arm, his other arm wrapped around Beth's shoulder.

"Everybody's happy," he says. "We're all going to have a great time."

She hugs up against Leon. "I just got sick of waiting here on New Year's Eve. I thought you had forgotten all about me."

"It's my fault," I say. "You get me into a strip show, and it's hard to...."

I notice Leon kind of grimacing at me.

"Strip show? Strip show, Leon?" She takes his arm off her shoulder, holding his wrist in both her hands like she's about to do a judo move, and then drops the arm and heads for the bedroom again. A door slams.

"Uh oh," I say. "She didn't know?"

"Thanks," Leon says. He sets Ron down and goes after her. Loud voices come from their bedroom.

I sink down into a rocking chair. It's a big, comfortable den, filled with Ron's toys. I keep promising to help Leon put in a fireplace, but we never get around to it. Every time I come here, Beth will end up making some crack about the fireplace we've never built. It's stuff like that that makes me want to get her goat. But I shouldn't have mentioned the strip show. I just wanted to tease her a little. I didn't know she'd be so sensitive about it.

Ron kneels down on the brown carpet, heels tucked beneath his pint-sized buttocks, staring at the blank TV screen. He's wearing flannel pajamas with bears on them, riding bikes, juggling balls, smoking cigars. "How come the TV isn't on, stupid jerk? Want to read me a book?"

"I don't know."

"You want the one about dinosaurs?"

"Okay."

Without standing up, he scoots across the carpet on the seat of his pants, moving his arms like he's rowing a boat. He digs a book out of a toy chest and rows back across the carpet. He sits in my lap, and we rock and read about the dinosaurs, who are no longer with us.

"They got stuck in the mud," he says. "That's how come there aren't any more."

"There's still some in Alaska."

"Where's that?" He sounds concerned.

"A long way from here."

We turn to the page with the Tyrannosaurus Rex. "How far though?"

"Where it snows. I was kidding. There aren't any dinosaurs."

"I bet a Tyrannosaurus Rex would eat off your head. What about wolves?"

"What about them?"

"You know, Scooter."

"What?"

"Are there wolves?"

"Not around here."

"In Alaska?"

"Maybe. But they won't come here. If they do, we'll kick their butts."

The happy couple returns. They're not quite as cuddly as before, but they're working on it. They're holding hands. They go into the kitchen and come out with green drinks. Leon turns on the TV He finds the station with the people milling around in Times Square. He sits on the couch with Beth, his arms around her. I can't complain. I like it when people look happy.

"Mommy, Scooter said we'd kick the wolves' butts if they came here."

"Did he? Really, Scooter." But she laughs. This isn't so bad. It's fun in its own way. The people in Times Square are really jammed up, rubbing up against each other, swigging from bottles, waving at the cameras. It would be fun to be there. It would be fun to be a lot of places. It's hard to get enough. You need to be doing everything at once.

Then I remember the fireworks. "Hey, I got some bottle rockets in the truck. What do you say we shoot those suckers off?"

"We ought to wait right until midnight," Leon says.

There he goes again. You can't just do things as they come. You've got to plan it all out until there isn't any fun in it anyway.

"No, now Daddy. Let's shoot those suckers off now."

Leon and Beth are both comfy on the couch. They look at each other, not wanting to get up.

"Maybe you're right," I say, sorry for what I've set in motion. "Let's just wait until midnight."

"No, I'll be asleep," Ron protests and wiggles in my lap.

"Okay," Leon says. "We'll do it now, Superboy."

"Well, look, I'll take him out," I say. "Just for a second."

Beth gets up with a sigh. "C'mon, Ron, you're going to have to get your coat and shoes on, just so we can go outside and watch Scooter shoot off his fireworks."

Sam breaks off from his steam breathing and comes out in the backyard with us. We set the bottle rockets in soda bottles and light the fuses. They whistle up in the air, explode in sparks, and Ron claps his hands and laughs. I'm feeling a little crummy, knowing they didn't trust me with Ron, thinking maybe I'd be irresponsible and we'd end up having an accident.

Leon puts his hand on my shoulder and whispers, "I'm going to save one for midnight."

"Sure, Leon. That's great."

When we go inside, I sit back down on the rocking chair. This time Ron climbs up on my lap with an Aquaman comic book. Leon and Beth smooch like a teenage couple on the couch. We brought our noisemakers home from the bar, and now and then someone will toot on one and wave at the people in Times Square.

Ron glances up from the comic book. "Your nose looks like a strawberry."

"Thanks."

"Your breath is P.U."

"So's yours."

"Scooter?"

"Yeah?"

He touches my nose, which he has so kindly compared to a strawberry. "How come you cause us trouble?"

Old Leon and Beth are still kissing. They don't look over. A lot of years have gone down between me and Leon. Less between me and Beth, but it wouldn't matter how many years. We still wouldn't be easy around each other. We could explain our feelings up and down, and we still wouldn't get anywhere. I just mean trouble to her. She's built it up in her mind, but I guess I've given her reasons through the years. I'd take back some of it if I could.

Old Ron falls asleep in my lap. To tell the truth, his breath is P.U. Little boy P.U. coming from his open mouth, snot crusted around his nostrils. I carry him into his bedroom and lay him down on his bed. He's a good kid. I wouldn't want to be four again, having to put up with everybody's craziness.

It's getting close to midnight, and Leon has fallen through several stages and into sleep. He's snoring, head against Beth's shoulder. She looks lonely and drunk. The two are a hard combo. Sam wanders into the den wearing an air filter mask.

"What in the hell are you doing?" I ask.

"The dust is getting to me."

"What dust?"

"There's dust everywhere. The molecules in the walls are breaking down. The roof is breaking down. It gives off dust. Everything gives off dust."

"Why don't you move into an oxygen tank?"

Beth shakes Leon. "Leon, it's almost midnight."

"Happy New Year," he mumbles, without opening his eyes.

She sighs.

"Get tough with him," I say. "You want to wake him up? I'll wake him up."

I go into the kitchen, fill up half a glass of water, carry it into the den and pour it on Leon's face. He jumps like a cat, screaming, "I'll kill you!" He stalks around the den, wiping a furious hand across his wet face. He bares his teeth like a mad dog and snarls, "Out. Get out of my house."

"Hey, Leon, it was a joke," I say.

"So's this." He picks up a half-filled green drink and chunks the glass at me. I dodge out of the way, and it smashes against the wall, right in the spot where all these years we've talked about putting the fireplace.

"Leon. Leon, please." Beth looks like a nurse trying to calm down a wild man. "You settle down now, honey."

I haven't seen Leon looking so crazy in years. It's a beautiful sight.

He grabs a Coke bottle, and I think he's going to throw it at me. I'm getting ready for the old dodge scene again, but he stalks out the sliding glass door and into the backyard. He starts climbing up an oak tree that grows close to the house, the upper limbs drooping over the edge of the roof.

Beth touches Sam's arm. "Stop him, Sam. Leon, what are you doing?"

Sam mumbles something from beneath his mask and grabs on to one of Leon's legs. I grab the other leg, and we haul him down. We tackle him, and we all roll around on the ground like a short men's wrestling team. We pin him to the ground. Beth kneels beside him and strokes his hair. She's crying. "Leon honey, have you gone crazy?"

"I want to set the last bottle rocket off from the roof, honey" he says, sounding reasonable in a strange way.

"Why?"

"Because it's the last one, honey, and it's midnight. Let me up."

We ease off him, and he stands, brushing at his sweat shirt. He digs in his jeans pocket, brings out the bottle rocket, and holds it out to me. "You set it off. Go up on the roof and shoot it off."

"I don't care about it, Leon."

"Go on. Do it. Have fun. Get crazy. That's what you like."

"C'mon, Leon. Let's go inside," I say. "I don't care about it. Let's watch the people in Times Square."

"Shoot the damn bottle rocket off, will you?"

"Yeah, okay." There doesn't seem like much fun in it, but I start climbing the oak tree, Coke bottle in one hand.

"You be careful, Scooter," Beth calls.

It's funny. She can't stand me, but she wants me to be careful. If I got hurt, she'd take care of me.

I get up on the roof and hear bams and pops going off all over the neighborhood. There aren't any stars out. Just clouds and the fireworks streaking the sky. Maybe everybody feels like blowing up the neighborhood. Maybe they don't. A lot of people don't mind what they have. A lot of people don't mind being dulled out, if that's what it is. It may be the way to go. Tomorrow I'll talk to the guy who was washing his car this evening. I'll say, "Pistol, tell me about yourself, what makes you tick? What makes you want to wash your car on New Year's Eve?" Maybe we'll become friends then. He'll laugh and say, "Glad you asked."

Sometimes I feel tired. The trouble with hellraising is that you feel rocky and worn down when you stop. And each year there's less people who will put up with you. Leon still puts up with me. We go back a long way. Sometimes you get down to that one friend who you can't afford to lose.

"Scooter, shoot the firecracker off and come on down," Beth calls. "It's cold."

"You want me to come down?"

"Hell yes," Leon says.

"You're not mad?"

"Of course I'm mad. Get down here so I can kick your butt between your ears. You've been a real rhino tonight."

"C'mon, Scooter," Beth calls. "I'll fix up the couch for you."

She sounds tired. I'm a thorn in her side I guess, but after a while people can sort of get used to even a thorn. So I guess I'll keep haunting her holidays for a while to come. That's what I'm for anyway, so that when I'm gone, she and Leon can sort out the jumble and end up settling even deeper into their lives, until the next time I come to town.

So I shoot off the last bottle rocket. It fizzes through the air and sparkles down over old San Antone. Happy New Year to all, good folks and clods alike, to the rhinos and the dulled out.

I think I'll be good tomorrow. I'll spend a quiet day with Leon and his family. I'll help carve the turkey or something, and I won't put Tabasco in the cranberry like I did last year. I won't cause anybody trouble.

Back in Town

BEFORE I DRIVE THE WAGON into town, my wife makes me promise that I will not go into the saloon where No-Nose Ed and the other bad men hang out.

"Indeed I will not," I say, and I have no intention of so doing, for it has been a year now since I have given up drinking and whoring and looting and stealing horses and robbing banks and shooting up the town and using foul language.

This is a big day for us. The first day since I've reformed that I'm going back into town alone. In the bright early light, we stand in the doorway of our cabin and embrace like a couple of feverish teenagers.

We've been happy, terribly happy, and peaceful out here on the range. It is not always an easy life. The wind is high, the sun fierce, the soil hard, and all day there are demanding chores to perform. I am too wounded to do any of them, but sitting on the porch drinking lemonade, I call out encouragement and helpful bits of advice as my stoical wife goes relentlessly about her tasks, playfully drawing her revolver from time to time and firing some rounds in my direction.

It is often lonely on the range. But at night, as coyotes howl from the hills, we dance in the starlit fields behind our cabin, our clothing slipping away layer by layer, the two of us spinning and whirling in naked amazement, alone amidst miles and miles of sagebrush and tumbleweed, until we are gloriously joined together and we cry back in the starry night to the coyotes in the hills. And every morning I stumble into the high desert and say prayers of thanks for the newborn day.

Nearing town on the wagon, I think about how sad it would be to lose this new happy life, and I vow that there will be no drinking or whoring or looting or stealing horses or robbing banks or shooting up the town or using foul language. I will maintain my serenity even when confronted by morons which, unfortunately, occurs presently.

The traffic on Main Street, I see, has gotten worse. I'm stuck behind a wagon which has several blockheads in the back: young glassy-eyed men sporting ill-advised haircuts. They give me, my old wagon, and my tottering mule contemptuous looks as they spit over the back of their wagon. Their wagon looks a little too new and shiny and I suspect they've snuck somebody's old man's wagon out for a joyride. They whisper to each other and laugh as they spit in my direction. My old mule flicks its ears and turns its head back my way as if wondering how long we will suffer this uncouth behavior. Behind me, a hard pioneer woman with an anvil-shaped head shouts at me to move along. When I edge too close to the wagon in front, my mule's nose bumps into the tailgate of the morons' wagon and the young toughs shout and tumble out and start for me.

In the violent past, I would have whipped out my pistol and showered them with foul language. But I remember my vows and the image of my loving wife as we parted and I stand in my wagon, the sweat springing out on my forehead, my hand twitching on my gunless hip as I say, "You young miscreants step aside now. I know you're carrying all sorts of resentments about your parents, your lack of a classical education and appropriate male role models, and sure there's peer pressure...." But I can bear it no longer. I take a deep breath, preparing to release an explosion of foul language.

But at the last moment, I am saved by No-Nose Ed. Enormous No-Nose Ed steps down from the boardwalk and strides into their gang. Grinning tolerantly, he calls softly, "Now move along, boys." When they hesitate, he starts pinching noses and ears and they hop back onto their wagon, terrified. Their wagon rolls forward and I'm able to find a parking spot alongside the boardwalk near the grocery store.

No-Nose Ed stands beside my wagon, resting a hand on the top of the wooden seat near my shoulder. He looks me over thou ghtfully as I sit there, trembling. He shakes his head and whistles under his breath, "Looks like you were close to using foul language." His voice is soft, whiskey-cured. No-Nose Ed is a strapping man with a flaming red handlebar moustache, and were it not for the gleaming silver nose that's replaced the nose lopped off by a cranky deputy, he'd be a fine-looking man. Looking into his sleepy, sad, knowing eyes, I am reminded of how, when the tales are told, one person's villain may be another's hero.

"How you been, Ed?"

"Can't complain." The edges of his moustache droop sadly. "Drinking too much coffee, I guess. It gives me a rush, but then I drop." He holds out a hand which trembles faintly. "Makes it hard to shoot."

"Have you tried decaf?"

His eyes perk up. "Hey, come into the saloon for a whiskey."

"Sorry, Ed. I gave it all up."

"I know," he says. "And I'm happy for you. I thought you had a problem. The way you'd slur your words during a bank job. Hell, make it a sarsaparilla. The boys have been asking about you."

"Better not, Ed. Things have been good, you know. Me and the wife. It's a good quiet life."

He nods sadly and pats me on the shoulder, squeezing the nerve at the base of my neck and numbing my arm. He gives a sleepy wave and backs across the sandy street to the saloon, calling, "You'll get tired of it, you know. I tried."

He disappears through the swinging doors of the saloon. I'm sweating. A thin cold sheen has broken out all over me. I go into the store and do my shopping, lots of denim and fatback, and I load it all in the back of the wagon and tie it down. By then it is late afternoon with a hint of evening settling over the town, and I have no intention of going into the saloon, but I hear the music.

It's not the music from the saloon so much as it is that music I hear in my head sometimes, some faint and unbidden music which rises forth and makes me tilt my head in wonder. Trying to escape it, I stumble down an alleyway with overflowing trashcans. But the music grows louder, the tinselly plinking saloon piano transforming into a symphony of violins that stirs some ancient longing, driving me back onto the boardwalk and across the street into the saloon where I find myself standing at the bar ordering a sarsaparilla.

No-Nose Ed, standing at the far end of the crowded bar, lifts his glass in a toast and smiles at me. He winks at the bartender and when the bartender sets the glass before me, it is not sarsaparilla but whiskey. To my own disbelief, I drain it at a gulp. A hot white flash explodes in the back of my head and I gasp and start for the swinging doors of the saloon, but I'm called back by a chorus of laughter and music. I turn to see Ed drifting my way through clouds of smoke. I have a fleeting image of my wife; then I am walking calmly to meet Ed at the bar and another whiskey is already set in place. It goes down smoother than the first and the symphony recedes into a pleasant backdrop, the evening casts a melancholy reddish glow across the bar, and a voice inside my head says, "How you been?" A warm welcome back from a journey, a worthy one, to be recalled on nostalgic occasions but for the most part, best forgotten.

No-Nose is touching my elbow gently. "We've got a bank job tonight," he says, in the calm way you might understate good news.

"No bank job, Ed. I'm going to have a couple of drinks and get home to my wife. No bank job."

He nods kindly. "Relax. I'll make sure you're not included. Have you met my friend Pearl? She's a college student." He's signalling over a young woman wearing a red dress which is low at the breasts and high at the thighs. Her eyes are green, her hair auburn, and she tilts her chin and smiles at me. No-Nose Ed grins at me and says, "Enjoy. It supports her education."

"I'm married, Ed," I whisper. "I'm doing a little drinking for old time's sake, but I won't go whoring."

"Of course not. You're a better man than that."

He's moving away from me, waving a hand over his shoulder,

and before I can move Pearl has linked her arm in mine and is leaning her ample, mostly bare bosom against my shoulder; her long auburn hair brushes against my cheek. I know that I will not go upstairs with her, so for old time's sake we drink and laugh as I tell her tales of my ebullient past with No-Nose Ed and the boys before my recovery.

Her eyes look bright and misty as she listens. "You boys are bad," she says. "All the men at my school ever do is read and write poetry."

"That's terrible," I say. "Hell, when I was their age.... They ought to be out robbing banks."

Soon we are standing over the piano and singing and when I think to look, the sky above the swinging doors has grown black; for a moment I yearn to be in my wagon and on the road to home and my wife. Pearl tightens her grip on my arm and tilts her chin and her look now is a command. I press my lips to hers and her tongue is in my mouth and her hand slips behind my neck and holds me sternly.

"I ought to...be getting home...."

I've never looked into such shiny forceful green eyes. This college student could lead troops. She's captured my arm and we're walking up the stairs to the rooms above. I catch sight of Ed standing at the bar. Drink in hand, he looks our way and gives a soft smile and raises the fingers of one hand to his brow in his sleepy, sad wave.

As beautiful as she is, in bed I move more from memory than from passion, and afterwards she cannot touch my thudding, sinking heart. I've gone drinking today and I've gone whoring, and I must be on my way home to reclaim my new and happy life. I'll tell my wife...I'll tell her the wagon broke down. The wagon wheel rolled into a ditch, I'll tell her. I took in a Mass and had too much communion wine, I'll tell her, you know the way that Father Bill forces the chalice at you. You've got to believe me, I'll say, would I lie?

I'm pulling up my boots as Pearl sprawls amidst the rumpled sheets. "I want to see you again," she says, sitting up with the sheet drawn about her waist, her heavy round breasts exposed.

"Oh, Pearl," I say miserably. "My wife...."

Her green eyes fix me with a look at once icy and smoky. "Oh sure, the wife," she says bitterly. "Let's bring the wife into it now, shall we? Just what did you think you were doing if you were so concerned about the wife?"

I move over by the door and hang my head. "I didn't think, I guess."

"Well, I'll tell you what, mister. I think you did think. I think you did think plenty."

Pearl's face has turned red and pinched looking, and despite her nudity, she ominously reminds me of Sister Bernadette, my eighth-grade teacher.

"Did you think I was just some cheap prostitute or what?"

"Of course not."

"Oh, so you didn't think I was a prostitute? You didn't realize I was a prostitute? I was just some stupid college girl you were going to impress with your wicked tales, which, by the way, aren't nearly as wicked as you'd like to believe. You were going to use me and ride off laughing about it. Weren't you?"

"Not exactly."

"Not exactly," she mimics, wiggling her shoulders and breasts in a taunting gesture. "Then what exactly were you thinking? I want an answer to this question now: What is it that makes a married man, a happily married man, let's say, what makes a happily married man sleep with another woman?" From beneath her pillow, she draws out a silver derringer and aims it at my heart. "And it better be an honest answer. What is it? It is lust?"

"Well, there might be some of that in there."

"Is it pride? Showing off? The need to prove something?"

"Well, there might be some of that in there too. It's more like a feeling of losing control, of being dragged along by some kind of demon."

She laughs savagely, almost hysterically. "Who's dragging who, cowboy? You have your fun and when it's all over you moan and groan and want everybody to forgive you. You want to believe it's some kind of demon that drags you along, but you like the demon, rawhide; face it, you like it."

"Well thank you," I say. "Thank you for the twenty dollar analysis session."

She fires, grazing my head and knocking me back against the door. "Now get out, you rattlesnake!" she screams. "Before I use foul language!"

Clutching my bloody head, I lurch down the stairs. When I get to the bar, I see there's a fight going on. Chairs are flying everywhere, people are milling and swirling around, a few men are lying around looking dead, and No-Nose Ed, a sleepy smile on his face, is holding a gun to the piano player's head and inviting him to play on through the wreckage.

Perhaps it's my wounded head and the tinselly plinking piano that sets off again those terrible, symphonic strains here amidst the wreckage, over the breaking and smashing of chairs. I think of red shawls on the pale shoulders of women. I think of a sword rising from a lake. I think suddenly of my wife, the two of us dancing on the moonlit prairie behind our cabin. I must get to my wagon. I must clear my head and get to my wagon and be off. I must steer my wagon home to the woman who loves me; steer my wagon to the new happy life I have built.

Some of the boys go over to the bar to loot the whiskey, and it is a kind of grief that catapults me over the bar with them, makes me coldcock the bartender and help the boys make off with the whiskey. The boys and I run out the swinging saloon doors with our looted whiskey and the boys start untying their horses from the hitching post.

No-Nose Ed is beside me now, breathing his warm breath softly in my ear, taking my elbow gently and steering me towards a horse, a great black mare. "That's a good one," he says.

"I don't steal horses anymore," I say.

"Borrow it," he advises. "Here, you might need this."

He slips a gun in my waistband and I mount the horse. The horse rears, kicking its legs in the air, and I know I have found a fast one. We draw our guns and shoot up the town, first stopping quickly across the street to rob the bank.

And we are off across the plains, shouting and firing our pistols in the air. It is a glorious symphony, the shouting, the gunfire, the horses' hooves thundering across the plains and I know then that I am lost. I raise my chin to the sky, open my mouth, and release a torrent of pent-up foul language.

The shooting dies down. The hoofbeats slow. The horses come to a standstill. There is a sudden silence. The boys sit on their horses in a circle around me. No-Nose Ed clears his throat. Someone spits tobacco. A horse whinnies.

No-Nose Ed sits astride his horse like a huge solemn shadow. Finally he says, a little embarrassed, "There's no call for foul language. Not in this gang."

"I'm sorry," I say. "I got carried away."

He shrugs his shoulders, a movement infinitely slow, contained, measured, and somehow reassuring. Slowly he aims his pistol at my chest. With great care, he fires a bullet into my heart.

Ed puts his pistol back in his holster. "Okay, let's ride," he says, "if you've learned your lesson."

In death, I ride sadly along beside the boys, our horses' hooves beating out a ghostly tattoo as we gallop across the moonlit prairie.

The Dishwasher

I'M A DISHWASHER IN A RESTAURANT. I'm not trying to impress anybody. I'm not bragging. It's just what I do. It's not the glamorous job people make it out to be. Sure, you make a lot of dough and everybody looks up to you and respects you, but then again there's a lot of responsibility. It weighs on you. It wears on you. Everybody wants to be a dishwasher these days, I guess, but they've got an idealistic view of it.

"C'mon kid, c'mon kid, hustle, hustle, move 'em," the manager's calling in that friendly, staccato voice of his, pushing me on. "Move 'em kid, rinse that crap off, kid, first into the side sink, we don't want all that grease and stuff in the main sink, c'mon, *hustle. We're getting behind!*"

The waiters, waitresses, cook, are there now too, right behind him, cheering me on.

"C'mon, we need some silverware, we need some plates, we got people waiting, they're getting fierce out there. Give me a god-damn plate for Christ's sake."

"Okay, kid," the manager says, "after you rinse off all that ketch-up and chicken bones into the side sink, throw the plates and stuff into the soapy water in the main sink. Let 'em soak. Now as they're soaking, dig in there, that's right dig in there and—"

"Into all that grime and gray-black sudsy water, sir?" I ask.

"That's right. Scoop for the ones that have been soaking.

Scoop!" He makes a scooping motion with his hand.

"I think this one's ready, sir."

"What's that? Egg yolk.... I see egg yolk on that, Christ, get that off."

The cook shouts in that cheerful, chiding voice of his, "You *turkey*! I got eggs ready, I got hamburgers, I got fries, I got onion rings, I got grease popping up into my eyes, but I don't have a lousy plate to put anything on. *Turkey*!" The cook respects me a lot, and knows I take it in stride. He mumbles and swears some more, but I know that's just his style when he's tense.

"All right, kid." The manager's bent over with me now. We're both bent right over that steaming, bubbling, smelly sink together. He's got his top button loose. I can see the sweat pouring off of his face. He's breathing heavy, but his face is set dead and calm now, though I know what's going on under the surface. I respect him for his self-control since he has a generally florid personality.

"Okay, kid, how ya feeling?"

"I'm okay," I say.

"You got your mind on something today, don't you?"

I shake my head. "I'm just getting warm."

"You don't seem like you're really with it."

A plate squirts out of my soapy, slippery hands. I grab for it, knock it back up in the air, it twirls, the manager grabs for it, and sends it twisting back up in the other direction, I grab for it again, but it slides through my hands like I'm trying to grab a fish in the water, and lands with a sick-sounding clang and breaks into pieces on the floor.

The manager looks at me and coughs. He sort of stares up at the ceiling for awhile, as if wondering if it's ready for a new paint job. I watch the colors in his face change to red. I know he feels as badly about this as I do.

"Thank God it wasn't a glass," I say, "those really bust into bits."

"Are you happy here?" he asks me.

"Sure."

"I mean, are you really happy?"

The manager takes a personal as well as a professional interest in me. I respect him for that. "Of course," I say, "who wouldn't be?"

"Okay, we're going to forget about that one," he says. "It was just a plate." He gives a funny sort of laugh, short violent bursts of air, as if someone is standing behind him and giving him bear hugs.

"I don't mean to be *rude*," Sally, the waitress, comes back to say, "but people are really getting downright hostile. Some fellow out there is claiming he's having a low blood sugar attack. Can't we at least get them some coffee?"

The manager breathes. "Okay, let's start from scratch again. A whole new ballgame. You give the cups just a quick rinse. Okay, just a quick rinse, and then you put them on that tray, and then you run them through the machine, one cycle, takes five minutes, you take them out of the machine, you carry the tray out to the front where the waitress can get to them. Okay?"

"What tray?"

"That one."

"Oh. The blue one?"

He makes a funny little sound again, sort of a cross between laughing and gagging. "Yeah," he says, taking me suddenly by the arm in an affectionate gesture and leading me to the tray in question. He takes my hand in his in a fatherly way and places it on the tray. He rubs my hand across the tray so that I will get a good feel of it.

"Hard rubber?" I say.

"That's right. Hard rubber," he says.

"It doesn't melt in the machine?"

"No. Never. This is the tray that you will use. This is the tray that you will run through the machine with the coffee cups on it."

"Oh, okay," I say.

We bend back over the sink. The steam rises into my nostrils and I give a little laugh.

"What's funny?" the manager asks.

"I think of Macbeth. You know, the witch's cauldron."

"Oh, you think of Macbeth."

"I saw the movie," the cook calls. "Pretty weird." He gives a high pitched laugh. I know he's stoned.

Sally comes back. "I'm *not* going back out there," she says. "*I'm* the one who has to take all the guff when something isn't ready. I'm *not* going back out there until I can give them something."

"Tell them some jokes," the cook calls. "Do a little dance for them, Sally baby."

"I just wish *somebody* would tell me what's going on back here."

"Look, we got some paper cups," the manager says. "Stall them, give them some water in paper cups."

"Water in paper cups, beautiful," she says.

"One time in Atlanta," the cook starts.

"Oh, shut up," the manager says. "Just cook and shut up."

The cook slams down his spatula, "You riding me, man? You want me to walk off? You want me to walk off right now?"

"Lay off, Charlie. I didn't mean anything."

"You riding me?"

"Forget it. Okay? I'm sorry."

"You can do the cooking, you like it so much," he mumbles. But he goes back to flipping the hamburger patties. The manager and the cook always have a friendly, lively, give-and-take. I respect their relationship a lot.

"Okay kid, how we doing?" the manager says, rolling up his shirt sleeves. He edges in next to me at the sink, and stares at me, intent, and asks, looking down now at the gray stinking water. "You want me to go in there with you? You want me to go down in there with you?"

I put a tentative hand into the water. I go down a few inches. Something heavy, with a harsh, leathery feel butts up against my hand, and I jerk back. You never know what's floating around down there. I take a deep breath though, and say, "I'll handle it. I'll do it. Let me just try it my way."

He sighs heavily. He looks suddenly tired and old. "Okay, give it a go."

And I do. The plates come back with ketchup smeared across them, chicken bones, crumpled napkins, bits of bread dripping gravy, cigarettes snuffed out in egg yolks, mutilated french fries. I knock the paper and bones and ashes off into the trash can under the sink. Then I give a quick rinse in the sink to get the main crap off, then I drop them into the sudsy water of the main sink to soak off any crusty stuff. I scoop back into the sink, pull something out, give a quick wipe, and then put everything on a tray and run it through the machine on a five minute cycle. The machine finishes. Meanwhile, waiting for the machine, I keep up with the other stuff, knock the crap off, rinse, soak, scoop, wipe. The machine gives a buzz. I throw it open. Great clouds of steam boil my facial flesh. Sort the plates, silverware, glasses, cups. Run the plates over to the cook. Run the cups and the glasses out front where the waitress can get to them. The waitress runs back, grabs the plates from the cook that he's just filled with food, meanwhile crying out, "Two fries, three deluxe burgers, one without onions, two chicken dinners, substitute peas for corn on one of them."

"Substitute peas for corn," the cook repeats scornfully. He doesn't respect people who want substitutions.

But I'm really moving now. Trash off. Crap off. Rinse. Soak. Scoop. Wipe. Machine. Remove. Sort. Run over to the cook. I'm moving and the manager's calling out in his staccato voice, "Okay, kid, now we're going, now we're going, keep 'em moving, way to go kid, keep it up, we're catching up now," and out of the corner of my eye I catch the cook giving me a quick glance and nodding his head approvingly. The kid's okay, he's thinking, the kid's going to be okay. Sally, hustling by, gives me a little pat on the shoulder. "*Okay,*" she says, "*Okay.*" I respect her and may be falling in love with her.

The manager's grinning now. "Okay, doing a good job tonight, boys, yes sir. We're starting to do a good job. How we coming on the chicken, Charlie?"

"Chicken's okay," he says, "let's move the potatoes."

"I could move the potatoes," I say, "where do you want them?"

"No, kid, that's okay." The manager calls to Sally, "Move the potatoes. How's the cole slaw?"

"They ain't going for the cole slaw," Charlie says. "Day cook put too much mayonnaise, I think. You got to watch the mayonnaise on the cole slaw."

We're *going,* yes sir. I'm hot. I'm really hot. I'm sweating and shaking, but I'm moving fast, and the manager even says, "Hey, slow it down, don't kill yourself."

"No sir, I won't, I'm okay."

You can feel it when a restaurant's moving. Everybody's working in synchronization. You hear dishes and forks rattling, grease hissing. You feel like you're beating *them*. And them's the customers. The customers are out to get you and you're out to get them, and if you make them happy, you've *beaten* them.

"Slow it down, kid, slow it down," the manager says. "Don't burn yourself out."

And then Sally comes back into the grill area, and we all know, before she's said anything, that something's gone wrong.

"What is it, Sally?" the manager asks.

Slowly, she raises up a silver spoon for all of us to see. "Greasy," she says. "Somebody sent it back. Said it was greasy."

She looks down. None of us say anything. The cook whistles and turns back to his burgers, flipping them slowly and methodically. The manager takes the spoon from her, and tosses it back into the gray-black sudsy water. "Wash it again for the clown out there," he says.

I go back to my dishes, but I feel sick and disappointed inside. Later though the manager takes me aside and says gruffly, "It wasn't your fault. Don't get down. It was a tough break. The wrong spoon, the wrong guy...."

Later, down in the basement, I talk to the famous old janitor, who is mopping with slow, steady strokes.

"You like it here?" I ask. "You like the work?"

"Ah, I used to," he says. "I liked the reputation, you know. I liked the girls that came with it."

"But you don't like it anymore?"

"Ah, now it's just money. Everybody's just in it for the money. And I go along with them. I take what I can get. But I always loved it too. I was pretty good in my day." He sweeps his hand around at the clean looking rows of canned goods. "It all starts down here with me, you know. I make a mistake one day and it's all up. Yeah, I'm tired of the responsibility. I think I'm going to hang it up pretty soon."

"What will you do then?"

"I'm thinking of getting me a condominium in Vail. I've got a hell of a lot put away over the years." He chuckles and runs a hand through his thin white hair. "I guess I did all right after all."

I watch him go on mopping, mopping with even, steady, sliding strokes that show me that while he has probably never been truly gifted, not gifted in the way I sense I am in my field, he has made up for it with dedication, reliability, and respect.

The Unfolding

"HE TOLD SHARON HE'S LOOKING FOR a whole new way of life. He claims being a stockbroker is immoral. He's sick of their lifestyle, he says. He despises television now, hates parties. Says their friends are shallow."

"Maybe they are shallow," George said.

"Can you *imagine*? He told Sharon she didn't stimulate him *spiritually*." Mrs. Brady gave a wheezy laugh and raised her asthma inhalator to her lips. "That was the last thing he said to her. After that he stopped talking."

"I never knew Gerald was all that spiritual," George said.

"He used to be an altar boy," his mother said.

"Well, he still never seemed all that spiritual to me."

George rolled down the window, enjoying the cool mountain air as he cautiously steered the rental car around the winding curves. The afternoon was crisp, the winter sun bright. George was entranced by the views of forested hills, rugged rock outcroppings, and sudden sheer drop-offs. It felt wonderful to escape from the bleak Iowa winter, even if they were here in Northern California to help his older brother. He supposed they were here to help him, but it seemed terribly much like interfering.

"When he stayed in school and didn't flip out on LSD back in the sixties, I thought we were home clear, hallelujah," Mrs. Brady said. "And now he's almost forty years old and he runs off and leaves his wife and children to become a...." A disgusted look swept over her. "To become a *nudist*, of all things."

"I don't think he's become a nudist exactly, Mother."

"You heard what Sharon said. They all take baths together. It's a *religion*—the Consciousness Church. Have you ever heard of anything so crazy? Be careful, George. I don't like these cliffs."

George yawned. "You know, I feel like taking off *my* clothes. The sun's so bright and warm out here. I just want to dance naked."

Mrs. Brady batted at his arm. "Oh you're not, George!" Her laughter was breathless and, George felt, bordering on hysteria. "Tell me you're not going to become one of *them*."

Her khaki skirt and square-shouldered sweater reminded George of a uniform, which heightened his uneasy sense that they were on a mission and that he was following a potentially irrational leader. Mrs. Brady was convinced she could talk Gerald into going home, and she had enlisted George's support. But George was twelve years younger than his brother and he didn't feel he knew him very well.

"Well, of course nobody stimulates you spiritually all the time," Mrs. Brady went on. "Your father didn't stimulate *me* spiritually all the time. I'm sure I didn't stimulate *him* all the time. If Gerald's looking for something spiritual, he should go back to his own church. You don't need to dance naked or shave your head to be spiritual."

"He didn't shave his head," George said.

"All you've got to do is say one Hail Mary every day—one *good* Hail Mary—and God will listen. God doesn't expect us to carry on like holy rollers all the time. He doesn't work that way."

The back tires skidded on the shoulder gravel.

"Don't drive off the cliff just because I mentioned God. You're going to come to your senses one day. There are no atheists in the foxholes."

George groaned. "I didn't *say* I was an atheist."

Tanned and relaxed men and women wandered the serene sprawling grounds. George parked in front of one of several large, ramshackle wooden buildings. On a lawn, a young blonde-haired woman, athletic, husky, was performing Tai Chi. Her movements were graceful and mysterious. Her hands seemed to be weaving a spell. A massage workshop was also in progress. A woman was having her back walked on by a bald-headed man wearing a robe. Two teenagers were playing hacky-sack. A man with a dog on his shoulders was riding a unicycle. Mrs. Brady took a long pull on her inhalator.

Along with other weekend visitors, who had come to enjoy the baths, they checked into the motel. Gerald had left a message that he would join them shortly before supper.

The check-in clerk, a friendly elderly man with a Rip Van Winkle beard, cheerfully informed Mrs. Brady that swim suits were optional in the communal baths. "Relax and enjoy," he said. "Mi casa, su casa." Mrs. Brady thanked him. With a wary look she followed him up the stairs.

They were placed in adjoining rooms on the second floor. George stepped into his mother's room. It was a monk's retreat, small and sparse with bare boards, a narrow bed, and a rickety desk with a vase of water on top. There was no plumbing. The bathrooms were down the hall.

"I wonder if they've made a mistake," Mrs. Brady said. She looked a bit mournful. "I don't mind…but seventy-five dollars a night."

"That's with meals, Mom. And the hot springs. All the soaking you want. In the buff, no less." George flexed his back. "That will work out the old kinks."

Mrs. Brady's laughter rose a pitch in hysteria. She fell against George. "Oh my God, George, what have we gotten into?"

George patted her back. "Try to be open minded about this, mother."

"I *am* open minded!"

George liked the sparseness of his room. The floor creaked under his feet. He parted the curtain. The bald-headed man was still walking on the woman's back, but the blonde who'd been doing the Tai Chi had disappeared.

He took some books out of his suitcase, hoping to do some work during their visit. He was on Christmas vacation after teaching his very first semester of eighth grade social studies. He tried to be understanding towards his hyperactive charges, but by the holiday break he'd wished he could have the loudmouths bound and gagged.

He was tired from the trip west. He lay down and read, but soon his eyes grew heavy. When he woke, the sun was low in the sky, and the room had grown chilly. He was hungry. He knocked on his mother's door. When she answered, her eyes looked puffy.

"This place really is relaxing," George said. "I hardly ever fall asleep during the day."

"I slept too." She frowned at the vase on her desk. "You don't think they drug the water, do you?"

"Don't get paranoid, Mother."

"I'm not making this up, George. I've *heard* of this sort of thing."

"They don't drug the water. Now stop it."

"Well, I didn't say they did, did I? I was joking. So you don't need to get so huffy. But it does happen. They drug you and get you to sign over your house."

There was a knock. Gerald was half in, half out of the door, and a tall, robust man with sandy hair was nudging him forward. George noticed that Gerald's short frame had grown plumper. His cheeks were rounder, the lines around his eyes were more relaxed. His belly looked buoyant under his baggy sweater. The ends of Gerald's bushy moustache lifted in a tremulous smile.

Mrs. Brady wiped her palms on her skirt. "Oh, Gerald." She held her arms out. "Give me a hug."

Gerald wrapped his arms around his mother and squeezed. He held her at arm's length then and smiled softly at her, nodding his head to convince her he was well and happy and justified. He embraced George. George put his arms around him. Gerald felt soft and warm and smelled of minerals.

The sandy haired man clapped his hands together. "Bra-*vo*," he said. "I knew you'd be supportive, Mrs. Brady."

Mrs. Brady brushed at her hair, dishevelling it somehow, so that a lock of grey hair fell into her eyes. She looked as if she might have just wandered in from gardening, to find strangers in her home.

The tall man stopped and took both her hands in his. "My name is Richard, Mrs. Brady. I'm a healer."

Mrs. Brady's eyes clouded over.

Richard boomed with laughter. "Actually, I don't know what to call myself anymore. I've been a heart surgeon, a psychiatrist, a podiatrist and a proctologist. I lived with the Cherokees and studied herbs. I spent two years in China with the finest acupuncturist in the world. Dr. Ling. He cured brain tumors with his hands." Richard tapped his head. "Sickness isn't here." He tapped his heart. "It's here. Gerald didn't come here a minute too soon. I would have given him three months."

Fearfully, Mrs. Brady looked at her son. "What's wrong?"

Richard clucked his tongue and chuckled. "Cigarettes. Booze. Hypertension. Three months. Another stockbroker bites the dust." He turned his palm down. "Su wa ho," Richard said. "Dr. Ling. The heart is empty. Su wa ho. The heart is empty, so we die."

Mrs. Brady stepped past Richard to confront Gerald. "Gerald, have you had tests for all this?"

Gerald's smile was tolerant, as if he knew she'd ask him this.

"He doesn't need tests," Richard said. "*This* is the best medicine." He waved his hands about to encompass the resort. "This air, these mountains, this light, this sun, the baths…the spirit of our community, the consciousness. Su lo wa. The heart is full. Fu lo. Fu lo. Full life, full life." He clapped George on the shoulder, knocking him off balance. "How was the flight? How does it feel to be in California?"

"Fine," George said. "Fine."

Richard laughed and smacked George's shoulder again. "I was born in Waterloo."

"Gerald," Mrs. Brady said, "If you're not well we'll take you to a hospital. You can't stay here. Think of your family."

Gerald pushed his tongue against his cheek and looked past her. He did not look repentant for having left home. George thought he looked too unrepentant, as if he'd been practicing.

Mrs. Brady held Gerald's bicep in a pinch and gave his arm a light, playful shake. "Sharon told us you wouldn't talk. But I said, I bet he will. I'll bet he'll gab and gab and gab. You were always a gabber and I know you can't keep from talking for long. Oh, I remember when you were mad your cheeks would puff up you'd try so hard not to talk. But if I kept bugging you, you'd give up and shout at me to shut up. Well, that's exactly what I'm going to do. I'm going to keep bugging you until you come to your senses."

Gerald's lips pursed and his cheeks seemed to puff up a bit. But he didn't speak.

Richard frowned thoughtfully. "Mrs. Brady, if I may take the liberty of interfering for just a moment. Gerald has lost the desire to talk because he feels that most conversations are a form of lying. Perhaps that will help put things in the proper perspective."

Mrs. Brady looked from Richard to Gerald, and finding no support there she turned to George. George nodded his head and moved his lips to show that he was on her side.

"I'm your *mother*, Gerald. I don't lie to you. Now you knock off this nonsense and you talk to me. Gerald? You talk to me, Gerald?" She jiggled his arm. "Are you going to talk to me?"

He gave an upward, prayerful look, lips sealed. No. No, he wasn't going to talk to her.

Mrs. Brady wearily patted his arm and backed away. She touched her hair. Another lock fell forward. As he witnessed his mother turning listless and disheartened, George cast about in his mind for something to say. He gave a chuckle and said brightly, "Well, I guess the cat's really got Gerald's tongue." He followed with a high-pitched laugh as the others stared at him. George swallowed and shifted from foot to foot and was saved by the clanging of a bell.

"Ah, Pavlov, I'm salivating already," Richard said, laughing, as he took Mrs. Brady by the elbow. "You'll love the food here."

"Shouldn't I change?" Mrs. Brady asked.

"Come as you are. People *do*, straight from the baths."

Mrs. Brady groped in her purse and then took a wheezy pull on her inhalator.

Richard laughed exuberantly. "Oh, we make them put on a towel or something," he assured her.

The sun had already set as Richard led them across the grounds. Bands of red light lingered on the horizon and shapes moved through the twilight and converged upon the dining hall. The bell clanged again. George whispered to his mother, "Let's be very casual. Don't get uptight."

"I'm *not* uptight. Why do you say I'm uptight? I'm not uptight."

The four sat at a small table to themselves as people with glistening wet hair and sparkling eyes chatted amiably nearby at their communal tables. Mrs. Brady poked her fork in and out of her rice. "I would like to hear more about this Consciousness Church that Gerald has joined."

Her reasonable, calm tone worried George, but Richard looked eager to reply. Gerald sat silent, as if they were going to discuss someone he didn't know.

"Well, we're not a religion in the way most people think of religion," Richard said. "What some people have problems with is that we don't have any beliefs."

"A religion without beliefs?" George asked.

"Exactly. There are no rules, no do's, no don'ts. You just have to be committed to raising your consciousness. You see, everyone is filled with a spiritual essence, but that essence is blocked up in most of us. Our community here provides a time to allow that spiritual essence to unfold. The unfolding will take a different form for everyone. Some people will end up totally changing their lives. Others will return to their careers, to their families, but with a greater level of awareness and appreciation. We had a sumo wrestler here once who became a beekeeper. He didn't want to knock people down. He wanted to raise bees. It was quite a sight, a four-hundred-pound man in his underwear harvesting honey. But what if he had never discovered that? Can you imagine his loss? *Our* loss?" Richard smiled at George. "A lot of people come here just for a visit and end up changing their lives." His smile was being transformed now into a serious mien. "The world tries to deaden us, you know. We pursue money and success and we're surrounded by so much electricity—

television, washing machines, toasters—*Su hi wo*. The soul grows old."

"I don't see what's wrong with owning a toaster," Mrs. Brady said. "I do think a positive attitude is important."

"Exactly!"

"I've always said: Have a positive attitude and say a Hail Mary every day and you won't go wrong."

"That's beautiful," Richard said. "That's incredibly beautiful. Mrs. Brady, I respect your religion, but all those rules, all that guilt. Religion should be a celebration, shouldn't it?"

"Well, it *is* a celebration." Her voice rose to a near shout. "But religions *need* a few rules. We're not smart enough to figure it out for ourselves so God helps us by giving us a few rules. He knows we'll break them. He doesn't expect us to be perfect. That's why He gave us confession. We need more than…more than just some sort of spiritual *essence*. What Gerald needs to do…what Gerald needs to do.…" She leaned across the table and poked her face into Gerald's. "What Gerald needs to do is to go home to the people who love him. That's what God wants Gerald to do."

As she finished, her face was red with intensity. Gerald's jaw tightened and he breathed heavily through his nose. George felt his own heart beating rapidly. He feared his mother's explosions. He knew that if she did not calm down, she would begin to throw things. She had once attacked his father with a ladle. Gerald, too, was given to violence. On a golfing outing, when George was quite young, Gerald had threatened him with a putter.

"Let's all calm down," George said shakily.

"Spiritual essence," Mrs. Brady snarled, further outraged. "Spiritual essence, my foot. How much is Gerald paying for this unfolding business?"

Richard had been sitting back, finger to his chin. He now leaned forward and held Mrs. Brady's hand in both of his. "I think if you took a bath with us, you'd understand just how meaningful our religion is. It defies logical explanation. It's organic. Mysterious. Just like your religion. Come take a bath with us," he urged. "After you've experienced it you'll know what I'm talking about. After we've all had a nice hot bath together and maybe a glass of brandy or two, *then* let's talk." He patted her hands. "I have a feeling that you're not as uptight as you sound." He smiled understandingly. "I think that underneath that uniform there's a warm, free spirit. How old do you think I am, Mrs. Brady? Well, I'll tell you this. You're not *that* much older than me, fifteen years maybe, so I went through the same kind of conditioning and emotional repression as you. And what I'm saying is this: you can still have sex."

His mother looked so frozen as she stared at Richard's hands on top of hers that George thought she might never move again. "Mother?"

Richard lifted his hands off Mrs. Brady's and waved his water glass. "You can still do *anything*. There's an eighty-three-year-old woman here who hunts with a bow and arrow and makes luncheon meat out of wild boars. I don't necessarily approve of hunting, but there you go. She's unfolding. You don't have to be a lonely old widow, Mrs. Brady."

His mother rose, staring into space. She looked dizzy. "Mother?" George asked.

With her chin tilted upward, she walked unsteadily to the door. A draft of cold air blew across the table as she exited. George tossed down his napkin. "I'd better check on her."

As Richard pushed up from the table, his good spirits seemed undaunted. He nudged Gerald, whose lips were quivering as he stared at the door through which his mother had left. "Time for a bath," Richard said firmly. "I'm sure she's all right, George. This is just a bit new for her. After you check on her, why don't you join us?" Richard chuckled. "Wear a suit if you like. Oh, there is one small rule. In the very hottest bath—we call it the temple—there's no talking. We obey the rule of Total Silence."

In the dressing room, men and women mingled about in various stages of dressing and undressing. George slipped off his sweat pants, but kept on his bright blue swimming suit. He wished he were not so pale. Across the room, the blonde-haired woman who had been performing Tai Chi was stepping out of her panties. George wrapped his towel around his neck and followed her bronzed, muscular body out into the cool night air. Her hair fell in golden ringlets to her shoulders. As they moved away from the lights of the dressing room, her shape became fainter. He followed her up a short flight of steps and stubbed his toe. Holding in a cry of pain, he hopped along beside other shadowy shapes. George was the only one wearing clothes.

He eased himself into the still, quiet pool. The night was clear and chilly, but the water felt wonderfully warm and silky. George looked up into a vast, starry sky, and his heart beat with the sudden quickness one feels upon entering an alien territory. He heard whispers. He began to make out shapes in the water. He saw couples, locked in embraces, heads on each other's shoulders, turning together in slow, harmonious motion, intently sharing a dance of beginning or dying love.

George slipped out of his suit and laid it on the tile beside the pool. He felt instantly lighter; his movement seemed more free.

His eyes continued to adjust. He made out Richard's tall figure. Richard appeared to be teaching Gerald how to float. Gerald lay atop the water with Richard's hands supporting his back. George waded cautiously through the water and drew nearer. Now he could tell that Richard was chanting softly. It sounded like, "Ka-po-ha-ka-wi, ka-po-ha-ka-wi." Richard looked toward the stars. "Spirit master, allow the cleansing to occur," he intoned, and without warning he dunked Gerald under the water. He held him there. George could tell his brother was struggling. He started toward his defense, but Gerald surfaced, sputtering and rubbing at his eyes.

"Ah, George," Richard said warmly. He reached with his long arm and held and kneaded George's shoulder. "You're just in time. I'm performing an Arapaho cleansing."

"I thought it was the Cherokees you lived with."

Richard chuckled and wagged a finger at him. "You Iowans are always so skeptical. The cleansing ritual is over three thousand years old and is very well documented. I'm only one of eleven white men currently authorized to perform it. If you care to do any research, you'll find my name mentioned on page seventy-three of the book, *The Hidden Rituals of the North American Indian.*"

George shrugged. He felt hollow, unable to compete with Richard, out of his element.

"God, I'm glad you both came here." Richard said, with sudden vast affection. "Isn't this a fantastic place?"

Gerald's moustache crinkled above his lip in a smile. He reminded George of a fat, shy walrus. Gerald seemed more vulnerable now. He looked at George with friendliness and curiosity, almost as if he might like to talk.

"Let's take George to the temple," Richard said.

"Oh no. I don't think so," George said. The thought of entering a temple, naked, seemed the height of absurdity.

Richard laughed. "Oh, come on. It's just a bath. A very hot bath. All we ask is that you remain totally silent during the experience."

George did not like the sound of "during the experience." But he could not resist Richard's determination. They walked and bounced their way through the water to the far end of the pool and mounted some steps. Leaving the bath, George felt chilled by the windy night air. But they walked only a few feet before passing through a narrow doorway into a small, dark, cavern-like room with stone walls. Clouds of vapor rose from a small, oval pool. No one was bathing, but the blonde whom George had noticed lay alongside the pool. She was on her back, her knees bent. Her breasts, the slope of her belly, her thighs, glistened with sweat. She seemed to be concentrating on her navel.

Richard and Gerald descended into the pool, stopping on each step to adjust to the water. Finally, pushing their chests forward, they waded in the rest of the way. The water rose to Gerald's chin.

As he touched the water with his foot, George realized why they had entered slowly. The water was scalding. He didn't see how anyone could bear it. But he could not back away from the challenge. He forced himself down the steps, exhaling deeply as the water covered his stomach and chest. In pain, he looked at his brother. Gerald, however, seemed oblivious to anyone else's presence. The ends of his drooping moustache lifted in a tranquil, beatific smile. His plump cheeks looked even rounder. Gerald submerged himself in the steaming water, curling his body, arms to the side and front, floating in a posture sailors are taught to assume if lost at sea. Like a huge jellyfish, he floated without movement or tension. His head came up; the creature breathed; the head sank once more.

A vase of flowers and an orange rested in a niche in the wall. Richard was staring at the flowers and the orange, breathing deeply, as if in prayer or meditation.

George was feeling such an intense heat that he imagined his bodily fluids were coming to a boil. Weakness and nausea swept over him. He wobbled in the water. He admired the woman lying on her back, her knees in the air. He stared at her round, firm, glistening breasts. He thought that he had never seen such a beautiful woman.

He thought his body might soon adjust to the water, but he felt dizzier as the moments passed. His ears pounded. The flowers in the niche in the wall were brilliant. He shut his eyes but he could still see the flowers. He could see each petal separately. He parted the flowers. He was looking through the flowers at a cool pool in a hidden forest. The blonde woman knelt beside the pool, smiling at him, beckoning. She held forth a bright, luscious orange.

As his face fell into the hot water, his body reacted in panic. His heart pounding, George splashed to the steps and dashed upward, out of the steamy cavern-like room, into the cool night air.

At breakfast in the dining hall the next day, Richard informed George that he had had a mystical experience. George had never had a mystical experience before, so he wasn't sure. But he was intrigued by the idea.

Mrs. Brady had boycotted breakfast and was moping in her room. Gerald toyed with his oatmeal and seemed anxious to leave the dining hall. George had grown accustomed to his silence and wished some of his students back in Iowa would undergo this approach to self-discovery.

Richard and Gerald returned to the baths and George brought his mother coffee and a roll. She was still in her nightgown and her hair looked quite dishevelled. George had seldom seen her looking quite so depressed, but she gratefully accepted the coffee and roll. She sat at the desk, nibbling and swallowing coffee.

"You know, Mother. I don't think our being here is helping. I think it's Gerald's decision."

She chewed vigorously, flecks of roll gathering on her lip. She pushed her plate away. "Well, what should we do? Should we just

forget him? Should we just let him *rot* in this madhouse? Or should
we commit him in a *real* madhouse? That's what Sharon wants to
do with him. Maybe she's right. Maybe he's gone bug nutty. Maybe
he *belongs* here. This is about as crazy as it gets."

"Don't fly off the handle."

"Okay, mister, let's just forget him. Let's just let him *rot*. If that's
what he wants, okay." She stood up and looked for something to
throw. She rooted through her suitcase and flung clothing about
the room. "The hell with him. Let him rot. He won't talk to us, we
won't talk to him. Okay, by gum, okay. That's what he wants, that's
what we'll give him. The next time we see him, let's don't say a single solitary word. Let's pretend like he doesn't exist. We'll see how
he likes *that*. We'll lock him up. Okay, let's lock him up!" She flung
her clothing against the walls, up at the ceiling. George told his
mother to calm down. She kept throwing the clothing.

"I'm mad now!" she shouted. "Now I'm mad!"

"If you don't calm down, I'm leaving."

George ducked out the door as she threw a girdle at him.

George wandered the forested mountain trails. Green-golden
light fell through the Ponderosa pines. He felt he could walk forever. He puffed hard as he climbed steep paths, and breathed deeply
and stared in silence as he came to points where he looked out on
the blue ridges of distant mountain ranges.

He supposed he should agree with his mother. He supposed
that it was terrible that Gerald had left his family, but he couldn't
help thinking that Gerald and Sharon usually seemed irritated
with each other, and that the three kids were rather whiny and
demanding.

He couldn't help thinking that Gerald was having a wonderful
time. What an existence! Floating in a pool, not a care in the world,
not even having to speak to anyone. Why did he, George, have to
go back to a freezing winter to face feisty and petulant eighth
graders? Not to mention their parents and the paranoid school ad-
ministration. How pleasant it would be to stay here and take baths
and hike the trails and let the answers to life slowly unfold to him.
And if the answers took years to unfold, so much the better. There
was, of course, the problem with money. He could not afford to

stay for very long, and after a few weeks he would undoubtedly be booted out, penniless, having achieved only a partial unfolding.

In the afternoon, he returned to the baths. This time, only slightly self-conscious of his slender, pale body, he stripped and joined Richard and Gerald in the warm bath. In the sunlight the baths seemed more casual, less mysterious. There were no intimate embraces, no Arapaho cleansings taking place.

Richard chatted for a few minutes, mentioning that he suspected Mrs. Brady ate too much red meat. It tended to make one inflexible, he said. He floated away and left George alone with his silent brother.

Gerald looked as if he wanted to talk. He opened his mouth and shrugged his round shoulders. George looked into his brother's face. Was Gerald crazy? George did not think he saw insanity there. What did Gerald want to tell him? What had gone wrong in Gerald's life? George realized he had never really talked to his brother before. Not talked to him in any close, confiding way. Naked, in the bath next to him, it seemed suddenly possible.

"Was it so awful out there, Gerald? I'm not blaming you, you know. It's just that we'd like to be able to tell Sharon something. Do you plan to go back? I guess you don't know, do you?"

George found it easy to talk to someone who did not talk back, who only listened. It was almost like talking into a mirror. "I certainly know something's missing in my life, Gerald. I know that. I'm not sure what it is. I'm afraid I've never been very spiritual. I've always been very careful. I sort of believe in some kind of God, but I don't even usually have the time to stop and think about it, or if I do I get depressed. I'm afraid my spiritual essence is all blocked up."

Gerald's face strained. His lip quivered. The serene expression that had been there the day before had faded. George was looking into a troubled face.

Richard floated back. "His life was dead back there, George." He squeezed George's shoulder. "Most people's lives are dead."

"What about yours?" George asked, shaking the hand off his shoulder.

"I'm a happy man, George," Richard said. "I really am a happy man."

And it seemed true, George had to admit. He'd seldom met people who struck him as truly happy, but Richard looked and acted like a happy man.

"People don't have to live dead, boring lives." As if to prove it, Richard added, "This afternoon I'm going up in a *hot air balloon!*" His voice rose as if he were already sailing.

"Oh, my God," George said. "Mother."

She was wearing sunglasses that hid most of her face. She wore a skirted swimming suit. The skirt dropped almost to her knees. She frowned at them and sat on the edge of the pool and adjusted the skirt beneath her thighs. She dangled her feet in the water and kicked slowly.

George called, "Why don't you get in?"

"Is it chlorinated?"

Richard laughed. "Mrs. Brady, these waters have natural healing properties because of the magnesium content. We once lowered a woman in a wheelchair into the water and she climbed out and took off running."

Mrs. Brady frowned. After a few minutes she eased herself into the water, but she did not approach them. She stood with her back against the side of the pool, looking out through her dark glasses.

George waded over to his mother. "I'm glad you decided to join us. It shows tremendous courage."

An elderly man with crinkled skin, loose chest muscles, and drooping buttocks gingerly pigeon-toed his way to the pool. Mrs. Brady's eyes followed him. "What's *he* got to show off?"

George laughed. "I'm glad you're getting your sense of humor back."

She took off her glasses and lay them alongside the pool. George saw that her eyes were red and puffy. She headed toward Gerald, treading water with her arms like an explorer fording an African stream.

Gerald's moustache drooped a notch lower as she drew near.

"I'm not going to interfere," she said. "I'm not going to argue. I'm going to mind my own business. I just want you to know that Sharon may try to have you committed."

Gerald's face grew stern and stubborn. His tongue pushed

against his cheek. Richard hovered at his side. "I really must insist you quit harassing him."

"You may be enjoying yourself now, but I know you're not the kind of man who can forget his family. You can stay in the water all day, but your problems are still going to be waiting for you when you get out. If you need spiritual help, your own church is the place to start looking."

"Cadillacs, rosaries, and pass the collection plate," Richard said.

"Would you shut up?" Mrs. Brady shouted at him. "You just shut up, you! I'm on to you, Gerald. I don't think you're crazy at all. I don't think you give two hoots about spiritual essence. I think you've just got weak and lazy." Her voice cracked; it sounded wheezy. "You're a good man. I know you are. These people will use you. They'll take all your hard-earned money."

"My god, you're a crazy old bitch," Richard hissed. "I'm trying to save his life!"

Gerald spun away. With choppy strokes he swam across the pool. He climbed out. Head down, plump buttocks jiggling, he hastened through the doorway into the stone temple that contained the hot pool.

"I've been very tolerant until now," Richard said, "but now I want you off the grounds. You're ruining all my work." He bounced away through the water in pursuit of Gerald.

"Come on, George," his mother said. She climbed out of the pool and marched toward the temple, feet slapping wetly on the tile.

"Mother?" George pleaded, but he followed her through the doorway.

She stood beside the pool, hands on her hips, staring down on her son. He was floating on the water in his shipwrecked sailor's pose, head rising for air. In the stillness Mrs. Brady's voice rang out: "You may think I'm a stupid old lady, but I know this. Every day you hide out here is going to make it that much harder to come back into the real world."

Richard looked as if she had fired a gun. He pointed to a sign embedded in the rock wall. The sign read: PLEASE MAINTAIN SILENCE IN THIS HOLY TEMPLE.

George could hear his mother's heavy breathing. She seemed not to know what to make of the sign. She looked from the sign to Richard, who was standing indignantly in the pool, and at Gerald, still bobbing up and down. It seemed to George that his mother was going to turn and flee. "This isn't a temple," she said. "This is a swimming pool."

She aimed her words at Gerald though he was submerged in the water. "I can't believe you'd leave your wife and children for a swimming pool. Holy, holy, holy, baloney. God helps us with our lives. He doesn't want us to quit life and float around naked all the time. What if the saints had floated round naked? Where would we be? This isn't religion, it's selfishness."

Richard tried to shush her, he put his finger to his lips. He cupped his ears with his hands.

Mrs. Brady's wheezing grew. In the steamy, vaporous room she seemed witch-like, her gray hair dishevelled, her skirted swimming suit absurd, her voice crowing, halting, gasping for air; she seemed to George magnificent.

"This isn't the Gerald *I* know. This isn't the Gerald who drove ninety miles an hour to the hospital when his son fell out of a tree. I wonder what Jake...." She broke off, coughing, patted herself on the chest. "I wonder what Jake thinks *now*. This isn't the Gerald who takes his family to Yosemite every summer, builds the fire, sets up the tent, puts...." She wheezed. "Puts the food in the trees so the bears don't get it." She stamped her foot to bring her breath back. George took her arm and tried to lead her away. She batted at him to leave her alone. As Gerald bobbed up, she shouted, "This Gerald would let the bears eat all the food!" Gerald dove under. "This Gerald is a seal." She pretended to be taking peanuts from a bag and tossed them to him as he bobbed up and down. "You're unfolding into a seal, that's what you're unfolding into. A foolish, childish seal. A good-for-nothing seal. An irresponsible, selfish *seal*. I know you hear me, Gerald. Gerald, do you hear me? You are not a seal, Gerald. You may want to be a seal, but you are not. You are not—"

Gerald's head rose from the water. "Shut up, Mother." He stood up and pulled at his ears to clear the water from them.

"Gerald," Richard warned.

Gerald trudged up the pool steps and walked to his mother. Exhausted from her speech, Mrs. Brady was breathing hard. Gerald put his arms round her. She draped her arm round his waist. "Why didn't you bring your inhalator, Mother?" he asked. He led her to the temple door. Turning back to look at Richard, whose face was now fierce with anger, Gerald said, "I miss them."

As Gerald walked out of the temple, George watched Richard's look of fury transform itself into an expression of awe. "Fantastic," he said to George, "this unfolding."

George looked at him uncomprehending.

Richard continued. "Now he's ready to appreciate his home. I'm so glad I was able to help." He held out his palms to George. "But you, George," he said solemnly, "you'll be staying. We have progress to make."

As George hurried out the door, Richard called, "George! *Le tu so!* Encounter true life! True life, George!"

Escaping into the sunlight, George walked on trembling legs past the warm pool, where he caught sight once again of the beautiful blonde. She smiled at him from the water. Was it a message? An invitation? Could they share some glorious union?

Mrs. Brady and Gerald were going down the steps that led to the dressing room, but Mrs. Brady turned back and seemed to notice for the first time that George was naked. "My God, George! Get some clothes on." She threw him a towel. As he hesitated, his mother cried, "George, don't be a *traitor.*"

His mother disappeared down the steps, and George stood, towel in hand. The woman was no longer smiling at him, but was looking at him curiously. It seemed to George that all the faces in the pool were now looking at him in this curious, shy way, as if he were a stranger from a foreign land and they were trying to determine how to help him.

"What is your name?" he asked the woman, startled to hear his own voice. He was even more startled when she replied, "Heather."

He nodded, wrapped the towel round his waist. "I'll call you," he said. He hurried away. He felt she was watching him to observe his progress.

The Yellow House

I TOTE OUR ONE-YEAR-OLD BOY over my shoulder as Peter, our realtor, leads our small family down the short hallway of the little yellow house. Peter's from England, though his accent has softened from years in the States, and until recently he's been as cheery and tactful and deferential as one often pictures the British. With our finances, most of the houses we qualified for were dumps, and Peter discouraged us from many of them: "Wouldn't feel quite right letting you buy this one...not really the right thing for you...not right for the baby...."

But at last he's found a nice, if modest, house we can just afford. He's brought us back for a second visit; my wife's already convinced, but he's developed a metallic edge in his voice because I won't make up my mind.

He pauses in the hallway to rap on the wall. "Sturdy," he says proudly. "I know how you feel about sturdy walls, Frank." (Not my real name, but he has been mistakenly calling me Frank for so many weeks now that I have come to enjoy being called this.)

He knocks again and I think I detect a fragile sound in the woodwork. My thoughts again drift to Mexico; our hard-earned dollars would stretch far if we lived in a palapa on the Pacific coast.

"This is your man, Frank. I say go for it."

I jiggle the baby in my arms. "What do you think, Tolstoy?" (Not his real name, but he has come to enjoy being called this.) "Do you think you'd be happy here?"

"Bah." He widens his blue eyes and lets drool seep over his lip onto the lapel of my windbreaker.

"I appreciate your candor, Tolstoy. Stick to renting. Let someone else fix the furnace."

"Oh knock it off," my wife says, chuckling from behind us. "You know you like the house."

My wife is a husky blonde with a kind, oval face. She is also a black belt in Tae Kwon Do, and while I trust she would never dislocate my kneecap with a front snap kick, break my ribs or cause me any other harm, she makes me uneasy when her left shoulder dips and stiffens as it does now. She's had it with the cramped apartments we've lived in for years, tired of moving from city to city, state to state. Now that we have the baby it's time to stop our drifting, time to settle down. I know she's right, but my spirits sag in this pleasant enough neighborhood of small ranch homes and faded lawns. I can't help yearning to run with the bulls in Mexico one last time, one last time to run free.

Ellen smiles as we enter the bedroom that will be Tolstoy's. Her eyes brighten; already she's picturing the cheerful mural she will paint, a scene of bears and rhinos, Tolstoy's favorite animals—we think. She sniffs happily at the air, but I detect dust and toxic molecular particles rising from the beige wall-to-wall carpeting. Peter walks to the window and parts the green curtain left by the former occupants who are still in the process of moving their last things out. Here and there boxes are piled up; my sense is of a family fleeing in chaos and ruin.

"Bit late in the day now," Peter says in the dim room. "But in the morning you'll get a lovely light and a nice view of the street. The baby can watch the cars drive by."

"How nice," Ellen says. "He'll like that."

"If the molecular breakdown doesn't make him too woozy to care."

Peter slowly lets the curtain fall back in place. He turns. His voice comes out a bit breathless and high. "What is wrong now?"

"Oh, there's nothing *wrong*. It's just that the molecules break down in wall-to-wall carpeting and give off toxic particles that might give the baby a sinus condition. Asthma later on."

"You could take the carpet up," he whispers. "Certainly. Why not?"

He adjusts his glasses—a black, horn-rimmed type. He's taller than I by several inches. I'm thicker, though, and I think I could take him if we went to the carpet. Could pin and pummel him. Though that might be an inappropriate thing to do to one's realtor.

Ellen's shoulder dips again. "You never said anything about wall-to-wall carpeting before. But we could take it up. Good idea. I bet it's pinewood beneath. I love pinewood."

A traitor in the family. I see that she and Peter have conspired against me. I must watch Tolstoy, see with whom he'll throw in his lot. We'll head south, find an adobe house with a couple of cottonwood trees. Hang a hammock....

Peter gives a sinister chuckle. "This is your man, Frank. At seven percent it's a steal."

Ellen floats happily into the master bedroom; we follow as the toxic particles encircle us and waft about our heads.

The bed is gone, but the imprints from the bedposts remain in the carpet. Soon our bed will take its place here and the years will pass as we live within the walls of this little yellow house. As my wife and my realtor exchange glances and the baby writhes like an eel in my arms, I am gripped again by the question that haunts me, the question that stalks me as I shave, sip my morning coffee, drive to work: Is this my life? Is this the life that I was meant to live?

Nearing forty, one becomes aware that one can't afford to make too many more mistakes, to take too many wrong turns. The possibilities, the options, narrow down. Choose one thing and it precludes another. In the nights I wake and lie trembling to the bone. I listen to the rise and fall of Ellen's breathing and I wonder: Is this my life? Is this the life that I was meant to live? In the darkness, I slip into my son's room and stand over his crib and listen to his mutterings and stirrings; it is a kind of awe and wonder and joy and sadness that makes me ask: Is this my life? I love. I am loved. Yet a younger me still roams the rugged foothills of Guanajuato, or steals through the night to the cantinas, called on by the ballads of lost men and saloon love.

Instead we come to this. A little yellow house. Perhaps it's the right move, the right turn to take. No doubt. On summer evenings the aroma of lawnmower oil and barbecued steaks will envelop our patio, call us to some higher purpose.

Shall I plant saplings as my father did when he slowly turned our dirt plot to yard? Those trees are tall and sturdy now, the grass lush and thick, the dogs of thirty years buried near the garden, their graves neatly marked with stones. Oh son of mine, would you be happy in a little yellow home? Or shall we take our dough and split for Mexico?

Tolstoy wriggles into his mother's waiting arms, and Peter and I wander out to the backyard and survey the rickety cedar fence. It's an overcast day with hints of an approaching storm. A breeze blows the brown leaves across the yard and I sink my hands in the pockets of my windbreaker. Winter soon. We shuffle about, look down at our shoes. Peter clears his throat. "We can't wait on this too long you know, Frank. It'll slip through our fingers. I know it's what your family wants." His eyes bore in on me. He isn't the most successful real estate agent; his tweed coat looks a bit threadbare, and I fear his concern for my family may be tempered by his anxiety about meeting his own mortgage payment.

But the moment seems suddenly soft and intimate. Now Peter's eyes resemble those of a therapist, and I find myself blurting out, "Have you ever wanted more from love, Peter?"

"Beg pardon, old boy?"

"The big splash, you know. The earth moving under you and all that, the stars spinning overhead, an out-of-body experience. Oh, it's all fine, you know. It's great. No complaints here. But that mystical thing? Do you suppose it's all a myth?"

He coughs once into the middle of his hand, gives a nod, eyes bright, moist. "Ever been to a pro, old boy?"

We walk side by side, shoulders bumping, back to the patio. Peter taps on the exterior wall. "What would you say this siding is, Frank?" he asks, feigning ignorance to get me involved.

"I don't know. Some kind of cheap chipboard, I guess."

He grimaces. Through the rickety fence slats, the neighbor's dog sticks its black muzzle and growls.

"I don't know if I want my boy living next to a brute like that."

Peter removes his glasses. He breathes on one lens. With his thumb, he wipes the lens clean with precise, circular motions. His lips twitch.

"My father didn't have siding like this. Our house was brick."

He holds his glasses up to the sun, sighs, puts them back on. "This is washable, Frank. That's the nice thing. Besides, it's only a starter home."

"Wouldn't a starter home be more suited to someone a bit younger?"

"People are buying later these days, Frank."

"Are they?" I frighten myself by the note of desperation in my voice.

He lays a hand on my shoulder, and I momentarily experience a feeling for my realtor which is not too unlike love. "They certainly are buying later, Frank. Grown people live with their parents these days. I worked with a man fifty-eight years old, just moving out on his own for the first time. Found him a nice starter home. People are living longer, Frank. Plenty of time to upgrade."

The dog forces its paw through the fence; it whines with blood-lust frenzy and claws the air.

"Could we meet the neighbors?" I ask.

Peter brightens. It's the kind of question a realtor respects. "Certainly, Frank. Good idea."

We walk around the side of the house to the front yard, cross a small yellowing lawn, mount one step and ring the doorbell. I wonder what kind of neighbors they'll be. Thieves? Eavesdroppers? Will they play their music loud and snicker as we stroll past with Tolstoy?

"Maybe this isn't a good idea after all."

"Wait," he says, touching my sleeve.

We hear a movement behind the door, and then a woman about my own age swings open the door and looks at us through the screen. She's pretty, but tired looking. I hear the shouts of children playing.

"Hello," Peter says cheerily. "I'm a realtor. I'm selling the house next door."

"Oh." She smiles at us. She glances back in the direction of all the commotion and chuckles. "Want to sell this one while you're at it? Kids included."

Peter smiles. He puts his hand on my shoulder and kneads. "Frank here is going to be your new neighbor. He was wondering if you could tell him something about the neighborhood?"

"Sure. Want do you want to know?"

"Is it...well...is it...."

"Is it nice?" Peter asks. "Is it a nice place to live?"

"Oh sure. Yeah. It's safe. Quiet. The people are friendly. It's just...you know...." She shrugs her shoulders. "We bought it as a starter home."

I sigh. "And now you're stuck."

Peter takes me by the elbow and steers me away. "Frank, Frank, Frank," he breathes as he leads me across the driveway and back onto the front lawn of the little yellow house. "Frank, what is this attitude of yours?"

"I'm just trying to get to the truth, Peter. If we make the wrong choice now...."

"Frank." He grips both my elbows, looks me in the face, his eyes glinty beneath the thick glasses. "Courage, Frank. These are nothing but ordinary pre-sale jitters. Stay the course, man. Remember the purpose. A *home*. For Ellen. For the *baby*."

But as he holds me I suddenly realize what it is that I want. Not a home, not a family, not love.... What I want at the moment is loneliness, sheer hurting loneliness. The kind of loneliness that burns out the old self, that sets one aspin in the universe, free to be broken and made anew.

I pull my arms free. "I'm not buying it."

As I take off walking, I have a recollection of a long-ago argument with my father, when I left him standing in the yard in a hurt, abandoned pose such as Peter's. My father held out his hand to me and then let it drop in despair, as Peter does now. But I must not think of anyone else's hurt now. I must think only of my own escape. I am leaving, I am leaving, I am going to look for my new life.

Within two blocks, it occurs to me that this may not be the best place to begin searching for my new life. The neighborhood makes my spirits sink—the houses huddled on leaf-strewn lawns, teenagers on a front stoop casting sullen, dulled-out glances my way, a muddy drainage ditch in sight across a weedy vacant lot—a breeding ground for plague-carrying rodents. To the west, the sky has darkened to stormy black. By the next block, a squall descends, the wind whipping rain against the back of my neck. I raise the collar of my windbreaker and hurry on.

Then Peter toots his horn and pulls up beside me. Ellen's on the passenger side, her shoulder ominously dipped and stiffened. Tolstoy's tucked into the carseat in back, his face turned toward me, eyes wide, astonished.

I pick up my pace as Peter rolls alongside me, driving on the wrong side of the quiet street so he can talk out the window. "They're hot to trot, old man. They need to unload fast. We'll go for blood and ask for a point."

"You'll have to catch me first."

Ellen looks anxiously at me and Tolstoy stretches out a drooly hand and grins, and I know that I am already caught.

But I give a crazy laugh, crying out, "Catch me!" as I take off running down the sidewalk through the downpour.

Peter keeps tooting his horn, a melodious sound as they roll alongside me. The rain drenches me, runs down my neck; cold and clean, it revives me. Peter calls out his window, "I won't let you pass this up! You're going to love it here once you get used to it!"

I cut down an alleyway, but when I come to the other end Peter's car charges up like a determined, feisty bull. "Steady, man! Stay the course. Build up your equity!"

I dodge across a yard, hurdle a rose bush, trip on soggy turf, throw something in my knee. I stagger on, running for my life....

It is a snowy afternoon. I'm watching the Sunday football game with Peter, who has dropped by with a housewarming gift. Peter and I are settled on the couch while Tolstoy pulls himself up in front of the livingroom window to watch the cars pass. After a halfback makes a broken field run, Peter confides sadly, "Now that I've discovered American football, I've lost all interest in rugby." I pat his knee firmly. "Steady, man," I say. From down the hallway, we hear Ellen's tools clang and knock about as she takes up the beige carpeting. I think I detect the faint romantic scent of pine, mingling with the toxic molecular particles which rise gloriously about our heads and engulf us.

My Life as a Judo Master

WHEN I WAS EIGHT, though I had never taken a single lesson, I discovered that I was a judo master. My gift was revealed to me shortly after my family moved across town when, during my first week at my new school, I was attacked in the corridor by John Mattheny, a boy whom I'd had a harrowing experience with back in kindergarten. He was a husky little boy, a budding sociopath, and to everyone's amazement—my own, my classmates', and John's— when he grabbed me I pivoted and neatly flipped him over my shoulder, dropping him to the linoleum floor with an impressive thud.

The kindergarten, where my troubles with John had started years before, was run by Brigidine nuns and located on their convent grounds. Originally a Spanish fortress, the convent was surrounded by a thick rock wall. Inside the wall, on the vast grounds, there was a small school building made of brick; behind the school, down a long grassy path the sisters sometimes took us on, there was a tropical garden and old colonial adobe buildings, a chapel, and the nuns' residence.

A curious shadowy image rises from the deep: I see myself wandering alone, lost, through the nuns' house; there's a maze of dimly lit hallways and doors. I open a door and find a nun (I assume) sitting in a tub shaving her armpits. Her great pendulous breasts sway as she turns her head and sees me. In the image, the nun screams and rises dripping from the tub. I stand frozen in place as her beefy arms reach toward me. The image fades. I have nothing to tell me whether it is fact or fiction or what happened, but I am struck by my terror, my inability to move, to act, as her body, incredibly waffled and blue-veined, lurches wetly toward me.

We lived in San Antonio and, enamored with tales of the Alamo, I imagined that the convent, the old Spanish fortress, actually was the Alamo. On some mornings I was Davy Crockett; on other mornings I was a spy on a mysterious mission, or sometimes I was Davy Crockett who was also a spy. This was a rather mystical Davy Crockett who knew something the other Texans didn't, a Davy Crockett who was planning to get out alive.

Every morning I set off to fight a bloody pitched battle. Perhaps this concept sharpened the stomach jitters that overwhelmed me whenever my mother drove through the iron gate and parked in the gravel lot in front of the school. As she tried to coax me from the car, I clung to the inside door handle. A swarm of the black-robes emerged from the building, flung the car door open and tried to pry my fingers loose from the handle. Failing in that, other nuns took hold of my ankles and stretched me out like a rope. Their combined efforts, two or three prying on my fingers, two or three pulling my ankles, eventually wore me down. As my last finger slipped from the handle, I let out a terrorized sob and stretched my hand toward my mother, who slumped, guilt-ridden and teary-eyed, over the steering wheel.

One day I was hustled downstairs into a cave-like room full of golden statues. Safe from my mother's protective eyes, the nuns, perhaps sickened by my daily fits, pinched my nose and pulled my ears and pushed me about from one to another, my face seeking safety in the folds of their scorched-smelling robes.

Through an arched doorway, an immense nun appeared. She lifted me in her arms, drew me up to her face and stared with blue eyes that twinkled like chips of ice. I stared in horror at the huge mole on her cheek, from which sprouted long, thin white hairs. Spastically I sucked in air; voiceless, I fainted.

To the smell of incense, I woke in another underground room, which was small and bare with a marble fountain gurgling in the corner. I lay on a blanket on the stone floor in a patch of sunlight that streamed through a sole window high in the wall. A nun, this one with a broad gentle face, stroked my hair. She took my hand and led me upstairs to the dayroom, the quite cheerful dayroom with balloons hanging from the ceiling and stick-figure drawings tacked to the white walls. The children were watercoloring; at my entry they glanced up. Some whispered or passed the disquieting news with subterranean glances: here was one returned from the dungeon. Each felt a shiver of recognition and registered an early lesson: the dungeon awaited all who dared.

The kind sister put paper in front of me and a jar of paint and dabbed my fingers in it. Sniffling, I smeared patches of blue on the coarse paper. (Some thirty years later my mother does not believe that I was roughed up by the Brigidine nuns in an underground room; she happens to be friends with several nuns who are indistinguishable, these days, from other women. They greet me with smiles and warm handshakes and appear to be splendid people, but in my heart of hearts I am still a little pissed off at them.)

My reluctant daily entrances must have soured the nuns on me so that they didn't object when John Mattheny took his daily nap-time strolls atop my head. Each day after lunch we spread towels on the cool floor. All about me, my colleagues, some twenty of them, whimpered their way to sleep with little cries and moans. In that time my eyelids flickered like a sentry's in the dim bluish light. Rising across the way, as if through clouds of blue smoke and dust, John Mattheny clattered toward me, shod still in his black cowboy boots. I lay on my side, wincing, teeth gritted, as he stepped onto my head and balanced there, the heels of his boots digging into my ear and my cheek. He bounced. I only lay there, unprotesting, imagining that I was Davy Crockett who was pretending to be dead as the Mexicans mopped up the last of the Alamo defenders. Nearby a sister slumped in a tiny toddler's chair, her knees stuck up in the air, a rosary draped over her giant lap, her broad buttocks drooping off either side of the small wooden seat. Her head nodded drowsily. She said nothing.

Could this head-stomping really have happened every day? So I recall it, though my mother does not believe me.

•

I was horrified then when John Mattheny resurfaced in my life in the third grade. The bell had rung after recess. (I'd slopped chocolate milk down my shirt that day, which had made the children laugh and think me imbecilic; my silent mopey stares deepened the impression.) The khaki-uniformed boys and the plaid-skirted girls were swarming through the corridor, hot and flushed from play. Just outside our classroom, near the row of gray metal lockers, Mattheny came from behind and pushed me in the back. I lurched forward, bumping into the lockers and sliding off and blindly stumbling a few steps. I knew even as the hands had touched my back, knew before turning, that it was my old adversary. I'd noted him that first week at the new school, caught him watching me from slitted eyes across the classroom, but I had not given him a name. I had not called him Mattheny, head stomper, booted romper. I had tried to deny his existence. We shall not recall that time, I had thought, that time is smoke and dust. His slitted eyes had revealed: no, we will not recall that time here; that time is lost to smoke and dust, but we know that you are mine and I can walk across your head *anytime*.

Shall I say that I was a child drawn to the dramatic? That I had a brooding, battle-worn nature? A misplaced man of action?

I turned. I turned in that hallway. Our classmates, a lusty lynch mob, ringed us and cried out with the inspiring compassion of youth: "Get the new kid!"

Mattheny was not tall, but he was muscled beyond his years and knew it. His wide face seemed rugged as a commando's, his brown eyes eerily aloof, superior. His curly black hair came down low over his forehead, forming a triangle just over the bridge of his stubby nose.

"Get the new kid!" the lynch mob exhorted.

As he came forward, reaching for my shoulders, Mattheny resembled Frankenstein's monster. It was as he touched me that I found grace. I slipped my hand around his wrist, turned my back, bent over and hauled his baffled, surprisingly buoyant body over my shoulder and dropped him to the floor. Flat on his back, he looked up at me, stunned but not hurt.

For a moment no one spoke or moved. Then a boy cried, "The new kid flipped John!" Other boys and girls chirped in, "The new kid flipped John!" I believe it was Jerry Rodriguez, the only one who'd been friendly that week, who proclaimed, awestruck, "Sean knows judo!"

The magic word was spoken. A dozen voices echoed: "Judo!" A new truth sprung into being. Judo! No longer jeering, my class-mates widened the circle, giving me space. I looked coolly at them, eyes rimmed and glassy with sad knowledge of secret mysterious killer arts. I bowed slightly and walked into the classroom and took my rightful throne.

The classroom buzzed; before the ringing of the second bell, in a score of ways the tale was told, the legend created, the myth made. Across the room, Mattheny glowered darkly, brow furrowed. Penny Riley, pale-faced Penny Riley, fragile profile to me, twisted her flaxen hair behind her ear, and the corner of her mouth turned upward, slanted ever so slightly, favorably, in my direction.

Penny too had reappeared from that time of smoke and dust. In the Alamo she had been a nurse, bravely tending the wounded. Once she had touched my forehead, laid her cool hand to my bullet wound, and had I not whispered to her my secret? The terrible secret that I was not like the others? That I carried within my heart a dark mission and an outside hope of survival? Perhaps I carried a magic pill that would render me, to all appearances, dead, and when the Mexican troops finished bayoneting everybody, packed up and left the fort, I would awaken? Had I perhaps whispered this secret to her? And what memory of me did she retain from that time of smoke and dust? Did she recall the sweater she had given me one Christmas years ago, the sweater her mother, my mother's friend, had made her give me, the magnificent black sweater with the white reindeers woven across the chest? I had outgrown the sweater, and we would not speak of that time of smoke and dust. (Though twenty years later, running into Penny again and having a drink in her apart-ment, I wanted to but could not ask: Do you remember giving me a reindeer sweater? We drank and spoke of Mexico, where she had been and where I was going, and as she twisted her flaxen hair around her ear, I wanted to kiss her delicate lips, touch her pale,

China-doll face. And when I finished my bourbon and slumped down her stairs, unkissed, setting forth for Mexico, I felt like a spy operating undercover, my mission obscure, my contacts mysterious, fleeting, and beguiling.)

Through kindergarten and the first two grades, I'd been a miserable, whiny little kid who didn't get much respect. I was a skinny runt and nobody wanted me on his football or baseball team. My big brother, older by four years, considered me a loser. My sister avoided me and my baby brother wept copiously whenever I peered into his crib. My parents resigned themselves.

I had a grandma and I called her every night and sang a song, and I would sing that song to her across these thirty years of time could I recall the words and were she here to hear my craggly voice break into tune. Whenever she visited, Grandma was amazed with our new house—so much bigger than the last—two stories, pink brick, white shutters. My, daddy must be doing so well—oh yes, we were a big happy family in suburban San Antonio on the edge of the frontier. (Daily Indian raids; bandits riding through; and once we had a rattlesnake on the porch and my father, neatly, with his hoe, cleaved it in two. Though in my travels, I have come upon so many Texans of a certain age who share this image of fathers boldly cleaving rattlesnakes in two, that I grow suspect. What is memory and what is myth?) We had a Chihuahua named Rawhide and a backyard ringed with saplings. The sprouts of freshly planted grass struggled through the lumpy dirt and the whitish clumps of colichi, and each evening my father came home and patrolled the yard in his suit, squatting and encouraging the new grass, tossing chunks of the ubiquitous colichi over the fence into the alley, muttering, "We'll beat this damn colichi, boys." My brother and I nodded grimly. And we were firm in our resolve. We'd win our war, marshal our forces against the dreaded colichi. (Though visiting my mother these many years later, I patrol the yard and yearn to see even one single clump of colichi, so that my father's hand, reaching down, might spring to view, and then his sleeve, the dark suit coat, and now my father whole and rising, winding up, setting sail toward the alley, over the chainlink fence, his last unconquered clump of colichi.)

We were young and brave and starting out in our new home and to my good fortune I was suddenly, miraculously, a different lad entirely—no longer a snivelling whiner, but a master of judo.

Quickly, I made friends. My strange powers extended to football where I was suddenly the shiftiest-hipped kid in the third grade. Even my intellect, rather discredited up to this time, soared. I could, Sister Matthew reported, read at a *fifth grade level*! Returning from a parent-teacher conference, my mother disclosed this news to me in somber tones, her eyes misting over as if this God-given ability carried along with it awesome, perhaps tragic, responsibilities.

John Mattheny kept his eye on me. He was, in a sense, not a typical bully. He was given without warning to suddenly laying his head down on his desk and weeping, his broad shoulders and back heaving. His father was a wealthy businessman and an ex-marine, and it was rumored that he made John do fifty knuckle push-ups every morning and run barefoot on the hot asphalt during the summer. Certainly John was strong for his age, a tremendous athlete. Every day we played football during recess and lunch and after school. John could throw long passes that actually spiralled, and running with the ball, he'd simply lower his head and barrel people over. To be tackled by John was a bone-jarring experience.

We were the best football players in our class so we always played on opposite teams. While he relied on brute power, I spun and dodged my way down the field like a pinball, and to this day I have seldom known such joy as in those early happy days of football when Jerry Rodriguez would command, "Sean, pack the meat." Down the field I'd go, packing the meat, as elusive as any judo master could ever hope to be. After school, we played late into the afternoon, and then I'd giddily ride my bike home, weaving from side to side as I pedalled up the long hill my brother and I called Heartbreak Pass, dimly aware of the falling light, the chilly air—the neat front yards and the pink brick houses I turned to battlefields and fortresses; cannons fired, men pitched off scaffoldings, while a judo master serenely disarmed whole waves of enemies.

As well as John's sudden fearful fits, he was not a typical bully in other ways. I'd seen him take a few good beatings trying to protect other, weaker third graders who were being picked on by older boys, and if he had some money or food he was quick to share it with those who didn't.

It must have been painful for him, though, to have me challenge his natural right to dominate. A few weeks after the first incident, he attacked me again. As before, I reacted spontaneously, hooking a leg behind him and pushing him to the ground. He was too impressed to even glare.

"*Judo!*" the kids cried again, any lingering doubts dispelled.

John and I established an uncertain bond. Sister Matthew thought that I would be a good influence on him and switched our seats so that we sat side by side. But she underestimated the power of his will. By stages, I lost my moral grip; I became a bad boy.

When Sister Matthew's back was turned, John and I swordfought across the aisle with our pens; we put our hands to our throats as if we were choking; with our fingers we pushed up the tips of our noses, making pigs' snouts. John giggled and encouraged me on to greater depravities. Once he unzipped his trousers, pulled his spindly penis out and waggled it about. I followed suit. For several seconds, as Sister Matthew drew sentence diagrams on the board, our members probed the stifling classroom air; we tugged, we twisted, we spun them in circles while our classmates stared in horror and awe.

Sometimes when John urged me to be bad, I'd shake my head and whisper, "No, John, no." But he'd clench his jaw and glower so fiercely that my resistance caved in. Despairing, yet gleefully, I swordfought another day, mimed choking, made my nose into a pig's snout.

My misbehavior was both manic and calculated. I must keep John on my side. He was too dangerous an adversary. And what of Penny Riley? Was she smirking this day as I cut up? Or were her lips pursed in stern disapproval? Didn't she see that I was only doing a parody of a bad boy so that my cover would not be blown? (A parody which I would relentlessly pursue, refining and heightening my act through a score of years; could no one glimpse my essential purity, see through the drunken death mask, look beyond the lunatic defenses?)

When John and I cut up, the class would give us away with its titters. How well I remember kindly Sister Matthew turning slowly from the blackboard as we sealed our lips and assumed blank, stoical expressions. Her soft eyes found mine and she sighed, so hurt to discover me in the early warning signs of coming dissipation and ruin. After school her voice more sad than angry: "I expected this from John. But from you, Sean, from you...." I begged forgiveness, offered fervent promises, cried into her black habit.

Yet all that autumn I soared, a master of judo, a football wizard, a fearless frontiersman, a spy with an eye on Penny Riley.

In the evenings before supper, I played Alamo with my big brother in the backyard. To my chagrin, he insisted on being Davy Crockett and made me be the Mexicans. He shot hundreds of me down with his imaginary rifle, but in the end he allowed me to bayonet him with a plastic baseball bat. He sank to his knees with a great moaning and crying out, but even as Crockett's life slipped away, he killed a dozen more troops with a rubber knife. My brother provided commentary as he died: "Crockett's bleeding everywhere...he's lost five gallons of blood...now they stick another bayonet all the way through him...it sticks out his back...but he's not dead yet...he keeps fighting...he gets shot in the head...Davy Crockett refuses to die!...the Mexicans are shooting the shit out of him now but he refuses to die!...they can't kill him! he's only got one arm left...he kicks Santa Anna in the balls...now they're aiming a cannon at him...." At last he howled in final death agony, shrieking so loudly my mother might lean her head out the sliding glass door.

All the while an inner voice whispered madly that really *I* was Davy Crockett, as well as being a spy who knew judo. But somehow, whenever I tried my judo on my brother, he got me in a headlock and threw me to the ground. I did not know why my judo mastery did not apply to him, but I supposed it was due to a character defect on his part.

We had a CYO flag football team, and John and I played on the same side against opposing schools. In flag football John could not rely on power. He was our quarterback and he liked to rear back and sail the ball high through the autumn air, and I'm not sure he cared if anyone caught it or not. When we won he shrugged his shoulders. When we lost he refused to shake the other team's hands.

One afternoon our flag football team went to play a game against Holy Rosary on the poor side of town, in the barrio. At practice the day before the game, Coach Garza, who had grown up in the barrio, told us that the neighborhood could be rough and he cautioned us to stick together and not to go running off to the concession stand after the game.

My mother drove me and John Mattheny and Jerry Rodriguez and a couple of other boys to the game. After she crossed Bandera Road, she became skittish as the boys talked about rumors they'd heard, how the men on this side of town carried switchblades and how they'd carve you up if you looked at them too long, or spat on the sidewalk near them, or talked to their sisters. You especially did not want to talk to their sisters, though why I would want to do so I could not fathom.

My mother told us we were imagining things. Then she told us to lock the doors.

She consulted a map and made a series of turns that led us down ever narrower and rutted streets. We fell silent. These houses did not look like our houses. They were small and rundown with sagging roofs and peeling paint. The houses crouched, close to the street, on tiny yards which were full of broken machinery. Clothes hung on lines. A group of men with thin dark faces sat on the front steps of a house and watched the passage of our white station wagon, and our own fathers seemed suddenly soft and round and harmless. These hard men, we thought, must carry switchblades.

The Holy Rosary athletic complex was a large one, with several fields and several football games going on simultaneously. We parked in a gravel lot. My mother kept her hand on my shoulder as we walked stiffly by some teenagers who were sitting in a car drinking beer. As our group shuffled past them, we heard them laughing and calling to us. My mother squeezed my shoulder, though I wanted her to take her hand away.

We found the field where our teammates had already gathered on the sidelines. My mother spotted some of the other parents in the stands and looked relieved. Before she hurried to join them, to my horror she kissed me on the cheek. As she walked away, my friends danced around me, hooting, "Cooties, cooties. Sean's got cooties!"

"Fuck you," I said.

"Fuck you, Sean," John said gleefully, enjoying the word. He punched my arm and skipped away.

My friends were distracted by the sight of the Holy Rosary team warming up. In their maroon jerseys, their team looked crisp and sharp and seasoned. To our dismay, their quarterback (by division rules no older than nine) was as big as Coach Garza and had a suspicious stubble above his upper lip. He was lobbing passes forty yards downfield. We panicked: "Coach, that guy's got a moustache!"

Coach Garza trotted across the field. It was about forty degrees that day but, as always, Coach Garza wore long gray shorts and carried a huge set of keys on his belt. He left the sometimes uneasy impression that he could open any door.

He conferred with the referee, who signalled the opposing coach to join them. Coach Garza waved his hands in the air and pointed at the boy with the moustache. The Holy Rosary coach kicked some dirt on Coach Garza's shoes and Coach Garza took off his visored cap to let some cool air on his close-cropped skull. He shook his head and trotted back to us.

"Boys, they say he's only nine. But we're not going to take this lying down. We're going to file a league protest."

A league protest! we echoed admiringly. It called to mind weighty men in white wigs who would see that justice was served.

"In the meantime, we'll play our game the way we know how. We're not going to let a moustache scare us. They put their pants on one leg at a time just like the rest of us."

We huddled on the sidelines, stacking our hands atop one another's and Coach Garza led us in a prayer that we would play a hard fair game, the kind of game, he implied, that God would be proud of. On the other sideline, the Holy Rosary team was praying too, but we trusted that God would deem our solicitations more heartfelt and that He would lend no succor to nine-year-old quarterbacks who sprouted moustaches.

"Let's go get them, boys!"

"Let's get them!" we cried, breaking huddle.

As we took the field, John Mattheny gripped my arm and looked into my eyes. "Those Mexicans are going to kick our butts," he said.

And they did. Their offense ran and passed for touchdowns at will. Their defense broke through our line and stripped John of his flags before he could even throw the ball. Once, rattled, he handed off to a charging lineman who trotted in untouched for another score.

I was playing defensive end and their halfback, a scrawny little bastard, took a pitchout around my corner. I slapped futilely at his squirming hips, the flags brushing through my fingers. As he cruised past, I put both hands on his back and shoved him as hard as I could. He crashed head over heels; his chin scooted along the grass. He sprang to his feet and shook his finger in my face, hissing, "You pushed, man. You can't push! No pushing!"

He shoved me in the chest and the referee ran over and separated us. The boy glared as he backed to his huddle. "I'll get you, man," he called.

On the next play he took a pitchout and headed my way. So did the rest of his team. They stampeded over me and I went down in a tangle of bodies. As the ref's whistle blew, the halfback ran over my head, his sneaker implanting itself on my cheek.

After the game, John and I and Jerry Rodriguez broke the rule about the team sticking together and ran down a hill to the concession stand. There was a long line of jostling boys, and by the time we had our sodas in hand, the sun was starting to set and the field lights had come on. I knew my mother would be alarmed and that we would have to hurry to find her, but John had seen something that intrigued him. Behind the concession stand there was a deserted, weedy, overgrown field with a few swingsets and a merry-go-round. "Come on," he said, and we trotted after him, our sodas splashing in the paper cups as we crossed a concrete bridge that spanned a ditch.

We charged the merry-go-round, an old, wooden, splintery affair. We set our cups aside and kicked it into motion; it wobbled and creaked. We circled a few times and hopped off. "What a piece of shit," John said, "that's all the dirty Mexicans can afford."

Jerry Rodriguez laughed, and I thought to look at him then. He had just picked up his drink; his eyes blinked over the rim of the cup as he looked away from us. I did not know how to describe the look then, what label to call it by, but I know now that it was a hunted, trapped look, a look I have since felt on my own face a thousand times.

"We better go," I said.

"This place is garbage," John said. He dashed his empty cup to the ground and Jerry and I followed suit.

We ran back toward the bridge, just as five boys were crossing from the other side. They came across the bridge to our side and stood blocking our way. The little halfback I'd pushed was in front. He was flanked by some older, bigger boys.

We stopped a few feet away from them and waited for them to move out of the way. The little halfback glanced sidelong at his friends. Then he walked up to me, looked in my eyes, and slapped me hard in the face.

My chest tightened and I stood there, feeling frozen, my hands at my side, as he slapped me again. John and Jerry moved aside to give me room.

"Flip him, Sean," John said angrily. "Use your judo."

I waited for the right moment to make my move. But my eyes swept past the boy to the group of smirking friends behind him—I bet they carried switchblades and the moment I touched the kid they'd swarm us.

"You're chicken, man," the runt said. He slapped me a third, and then a fourth, and then a fifth time, and there was something in his eyes, a shiny look of pleasure that sent a chill through me.

"Flip him, damn it Sean!" John cried, his voice cracking in fury, "don't worry about the rest of them." He moved in front of the group of five. "Flip him, Sean," he implored, "don't just stand there."

"He's chicken," the runt said. And he slapped me time after

time as I stood there. First he set a slow rhythm, slapping and pausing and saying "Chicken," before slapping again. Then he fell silent and slapped harder, his face darkening until he looked a little frightened himself.

"Don't just stand there!" John screamed, sounding as if he were about to cry.

My arms hung lifeless at my sides, but on the next slap I would flip him, on the very next slap I would.... Slap. Slap. Slap.

Then a voice, Coach Garza's, was shouting from the bridge. "What's going on?"

The runt put his hand to my burning cheek and patted it almost gently. "So long, chicken. Stay on your side of town next time."

Coach Garza came alongside us, pushed the boy away. "Beat it."

"I'm going, man, I'm going." He joined his friends and they sauntered off, laughing, as they crossed the weedy field toward the neighborhood that bordered it.

My friends were silent. I stared at the ground and felt their eyes on me. Coach Garza tilted my chin with his finger. "Son?"

I broke from him and ran for my mother's car.

Riding back through the dark streets, our doors locked, my mother couldn't understand our silence. "It's just a game," she said. "So what if you lost? It's no big deal."

John's voice drifted from the back seat. "He slapped him. He slapped him and he just stood there." He said it quietly, distantly, as if he wasn't addressing anyone in particular.

"Who?" my mother asked. "Who slapped who?"

"Nobody," I muttered.

Her head swivelled toward me as I died against the door. "Who slapped who?"

"Shut up," I whispered.

Her voice grew shrill. "I want to know who slapped who. Well? Who slapped who?"

I screamed, "Shut up! Shut up! Shut up!" and covered my face with my hands.

Word spread quickly at school. The next morning when I entered the room, the kids watched me. I tried to give them a cool look—a judo master look. Didn't they understand that I'd acted wisely? Kept the other boys from being knifed?

Sister Matthew wasn't there yet. I took my seat across from John and he wouldn't look at me.

Then the kids started in. From far across the room, I heard a single "Bawk." Then that was answered with a "Bawk Bawk" from the front row. The back of the room then pitched in. And now the whole class erupted in a chorus of "Bawk bawk bawk, chicken chicken, bawk bawk bawk, chicken chicken, bawk bawk bawk, chicken chicken."

I searched for allies; glancing sidelong, I saw that John was silent, his jaw clenched tight.

Ah, and there was Penny. Penny Riley, my old nurse. Surely Penny, my good nurse from the Alamo, would not desert me. A flush had come to her delicate face—her moist lips parted to speak in my defense. A speck of spittle had formed at the corner of her mouth; her features suddenly twisted and sharpened as she bent back her head, tilted her chin to the ceiling, made wings of her arms, and masterfully crowed, "Bawk bawk bawk, chicken chicken!"

"Shut up!" John yelled, and his voice was loud enough to bring a deathly quiet to the room, save for the last haunting strains of Penny's crow, which died note by note, until we all sat in the thick silence of the besieged.

Enter Sister Matthew, clad in black.

At recess that day we played football on the field behind the school. I ran like a madman through the crisp autumn air, dashing and darting and crashing through tacklers. I scored two touchdowns, but the next time I carried the ball, John grabbed me from behind, lifted me in the air and threw me to the grass. I stood up, heading to the huddle. Something slammed into the back of my head. I stumbled and felt a hot wave spread through the back of my head and neck and the wave turned to a sharp pain. Dizzy, I turned and saw the football still wobbling on the grass. John was facing me and I realized he'd thrown the ball at me.

I glared. "Why'd you—"

The boys were ringing us as they had that day just two months and a lifetime ago. "Get him, John!" they cried. "Get the chicken! Sean's a chicken!"

"Let's play football," Jerry said, but no one listened.

"Are you going to fight or not?" John asked. There wasn't any anger in his voice. Arms at his sides, he waited as if to perform a necessary rite.

"I'll fight you," I said thinly.

He nodded. We circled each other and the war cries of the boys rolled over us. He stepped forward and grabbed me by the shoulders. I clenched his wrist, pivoted and bent my back to flip him; he came halfway up my back and in a moment I would send him sailing and regain my rightful throne, except his weight suddenly seemed immense. My legs buckled and we fell to the grass together. We writhed on the ground and he ended up on top. He pinned me and slugged me in the face. I squirmed from underneath him and rose to my feet. He came at me again and grabbed the front of my windbreaker, tearing the zipper loose. I ducked my head and tackled him and we went to the ground again. We rolled around and again he pinned me, kneeled on my stomach, and slugged me in the head. Then he rested atop me, looking down into my face. The boys were quiet now. They weren't calling chicken anymore.

"Let him up, John," Jerry said. "Please let him up."

Slowly John rose. I picked myself up, panting for air. I looked wildly at John, unable to fight anymore, frightened to stop.

We faced each other. He gave me a long look and nodded his head faintly. Softly, a bit sadly, John said the most painful words: "You don't know judo, Sean."

My lip trembled and I fought back tears.

He shrugged his shoulders, turned and walked away, steps heavy, head down, as he crossed the field toward the red brick school building.

Then the bell was ringing. One by one, and then in a wave, the boys ran for the school. At first they ran quietly, and as they neared the school their voices broke into shouts as they heralded their return from yet another recess, as if, to them, it was simply another ordinary day.

As I straggled toward the school, I pulled my torn windbreaker tighter around my throat. I wondered what Penny Riley would think when she saw me stagger in from the battle, bloodied, wounded.

Crossing the field, I felt myself joined by shadows, the kind of shadows cast by judo masters, spies, and lone survivors, the kind that rise and wander, forever sleepless, searching abandoned fortresses for forgotten passageways.

First Day

THE BOSS SPAT. "Do you know how to work hard?" he asked. "I mean hard?"

"Not really," I said.

"I'll take a chance on you," he said. "The first thing you need to do is move that big thing over there."

"That big thing?"

"Hell yes, that big thing."

"It sure looks big," I said.

"You're goddamn right it's big. That is one big thing."

"Where do you want it?"

"Well, we sure as hell don't want it there, do we?"

"So where do we want it?"

"Where do you think we want it, Einstein?"

"Do we want it over there?" I asked, pointing.

"Hell no, we don't want it over there. What the hell would we want that big thing over there for?"

"I guess we don't."

"You're damn right we don't. Take it down to the goddamn warehouse, Edison."

"Where's the warehouse?"

"Where's the warehouse? You work here and you don't know where the goddamn warehouse is?" The boss spat. "Three blocks that way, and then turn that way and then turn that way. That's where the goddamn warehouse is, Balzac."

"Well, okay," I said. "I'll take that big thing down to the warehouse."

"They'll know what to do with that big thing there."

I got ahold of the big thing and tried to hoist it up on my shoulders.

The boss ran up. His face was red. He spat. "What do you think you're doing? You don't lift those big things, Galileo. You roll them. What did you do, go to college? You roll those goddamn big things. You don't lift them."

"Okay, okay," I said. "I'll roll it."

I got behind the big thing. I put my shoulder against it. I grunted. My heels came off the ground. The boss watched me. "How's it feel?" he asked.

"Big," I said.

"You're goddamn right," he said.

I dug my feet into the ground and pushed. It creaked and slid a couple of inches.

"Roll it straight, Da Vinci," the boss hollered. "Don't let that big thing get away from you."

It was getting easier. The big thing was starting to roll. The big thing bounced to the left, and the big thing dragged to the right, and I tried to move it from side to side. We rolled out the gate and on to the street. Cars started honking. People were yelling. A guy shouted out his window, "Get that big thing out of the street, you moron!"

I got the big thing up on the sidewalk. It started to pick up speed. It was really rolling now. I saw some people on the sidewalk. I tried to stop the big thing but it just pulled me along with it. "Hey look out," I called. "I can't slow this thing down."

"Watch it, watch it," a man cried. "He's out of control."

People dove out of the way. "Be careful with that big thing," a lady screamed. "You ought to be ashamed."

"I'm sorry, I'm sorry," I said. "I'm just trying to do my job."

I turned this way and I turned that way and then I turned that way, and I kept running behind the big thing calling, "Look out! Everybody look out!"

I saw a bunch of guys on the loading dock at the warehouse. They were hollering and waving their arms at me. The big thing rolled through the gate and headed right at them. They shouted and scattered out of the way as the big thing smashed into the dock. Wood splintered, some boxes fell, glass broke.

A man with a clipboard charged up to me. "What the hell are you trying to do with that big thing, kill somebody?" he screamed. Some guys with tattoos surrounded me and stood around spitting.

"My boss told me to take it down here," I said.

"Well, we sure as hell don't want that big thing here. Why the hell do you think we want that big thing down here?"

"I'm just trying to do my job," I said.

Somebody spat tobacco juice on my sneakers. The guy with the clipboard poked me in the chest. "You got a form?"

"No. Nobody said anything about a form."

"Well, I sure as hell can't take that thing without a form, can I? You're going to have to take that back and get a form."

"Okay," I said. "I'll get a form."

"And don't forget to bring me some avocados while you're at it."

"Okay. Sure."

They all hooted and whistled at me as I tried to get the big thing turned around.

"Crank it, crank the son of a bitch," somebody yelled.

"Where?"

"Where?" They all laughed like ruptured hyenas. "Crank it where?"

They hooted, punched each other in the ribs, slapped hands.

I stood on the dock and shoved and the big thing moved an inch and rolled back. The dock vibrated.

"Get that big thing out of here!" the clipboard guy yelled.

"Okay, I will," I said. I put my feet on the edge of the dock and leaned my back up against the big thing and pushed. It lurched forward suddenly and I fell off the dock and scraped my hands and knees. The big thing wobbled forward on its own.

The gang couldn't take it anymore. They convulsed with laughter. They collapsed and lay down on the dock squirming with laughter. One guy drew himself to his knees and said, "If you don't get that big thing out of here now, I'm going to waste you. I'm going to blow you away. We don't take that kind of crap here. We don't take it."

"I'll get it out of here," I said. I caught up to the big thing. It was rolling now. After it was rolling, it wanted to roll. It loved to roll. It was born to roll. After it was rolling, it would roll.

I didn't want to take the big thing back out on the street. I saw an alleyway. I thought I might be able to go back that way. I leaned my shoulder against the big thing. It decided to go the way I wanted to go.

We zoomed down the alley. We knocked over some trashcans. We scared the hell out of a cat. "Look out, cat," I called. The cat stared after us. Its confidence was shot to hell.

We rolled out of the alley and into a park. When the big thing hit the grass, it really started to move. I couldn't keep up with it. The big thing raced ahead of me. I thought that I had lost the big thing for good, but it smashed into a tree. The tree shuddered. The big thing sat against the tree looking like it wanted to belch. I ran up to it. The big thing looked okay. I was glad the boss hadn't seen me roll the big thing into a tree.

I saw a water fountain and I thought I'd get a drink. I left the big thing by the tree and walked over to the fountain. When I turned around, I saw two jerks rolling the big thing down a grassy hill.

"Hey, that's my big thing," I shouted. I ran after them.

The two jerks saw me coming and they gave the big thing a push and took off running in opposite directions. The big thing gathered speed and rolled down the hill and into a muddy ditch.

I slid down the bank of the ditch and waded through the mud to the big thing. I pushed against it and tried to rock it from side to side, but it was really stuck in the mud. It was starting to sink. I was starting to sink too. I'd gotten my foot caught underneath the big thing and now we were sinking together. I was down to my hips. Then I was down to my chest. The mud was up to my neck. I was going down with the big thing. I felt depressed.

"What the hell are you doing down there with that big thing, Houdini?" the boss screamed from up above me. He got out of a jeep. He spat. His face looked red. A tow truck pulled up behind the jeep. Some guys with tattoos got out and looked down at the big thing and me. The mud was over my chin. They looked at each other and shook their heads and spat.

"I ran into a little trouble," I said. "I was trying to bring this big thing back."

"Why the hell were you trying to bring that big thing back, Galahad?" the boss shouted.

"They said I needed a form."

"You forgot the form? You didn't take the goddamn form?"

"Nobody said anything about a form."

"Nobody said anything? You don't think you just move one of those big things without a form, do you?"

"I guess not," I mumbled. I had mud in my mouth.

"Get a cable around that big thing, boys," the boss said.

The guys with tattoos slid down the bank and looped a cable around the big thing and started hoisting it out. I held on to the big thing and they dragged me out with it. I was covered in mud. I had mud in my eyes.

The boss looked at me and spat. He signalled to a guy who had a toilet tattooed on his chest "Joe, take this big thing down to the warehouse and tell them I'm sorry for sending Sappho. Tell them Sappho just didn't know what the hell he was doing."

Joe spat. "No problem, boss."

"They want some avocados too," I said.

"Are you out of your mind, Columbus?" the boss snapped. "You mean you forgot the avocados? You didn't even take the avocados?"

The boss looked stunned. "Jesus Christ," he said to the other guys. "Can you imagine what would happen if they didn't get their avocados?"

The boys whistled and shook their heads.

"How could anyone forget the avocados?" the boss asked in disbelief.

"Am I fired?" I asked.

"Fired? Don't be so goddamn sensitive, Geronimo. Don't you like working here?" The boss got back in his jeep. "If you weren't so muddy, I'd give you a lift."

"Don't worry about it," I said.

"Get some lunch, Tolstoy." The boss spat and drove away.

I walked back to work. I sat down with some guys in the grass. They were grinning at me. They offered me some chips and avocado dip.

"So how do you like those big things?" they asked.

"They're okay," I said.

"You'll get the hang of them."

"Is the boss always like that?" I asked.

They stopped grinning. "Like what?"

"Nothing," I said.

"Hey, the boss is a great guy," they said.

"He seems like it," I said.

"You're new. Just listen and learn. You're going to love it here."

They spat. So did I.

The Pearl Diver

JEAN PAUL, THE OWNER AND HEAD CHEF of the fancy French restaurant where I work, throws temper tantrums. He is convinced that everyone is conspiring against him. The waiters write down the wrong orders, the dishwashers, or pearl divers as we are known in the trade, break glasses, and the other chefs burn up the food. The customers are cruel. If anyone orders a steak well done, he looks crushed, and then flies into a frenzy. Knife in hand, he looks prepared to storm out of the kitchen to dispatch the villain who would destroy a good piece of meat. "Tell him he cannot!" he shouts at the waiter. "Tell him he *cannot* have his steak well done!" A tall, rail-thin man in a white uniform, he acts like the crazed ruler of a beleaguered kingdom.

Some nights I amuse Jean Paul. I tell him that I am ranked the Number Two dishwasher in the nation. There's a fellow in St. Louis who defeats me every year at the annual tournament. I tell Jean Paul about my dishwashing techniques. Some nights I use a modern European style, where the emphasis is on speed, and one works with a cool, detached attitude. Other nights I try a Greco-Roman approach, tossing a saucer to Jean Paul as if it were a discus. When he complains that some of the pans are greasy, I tell him I am using an impressionistic technique, slightly under-washing the pans to leave something to the imagination. Just as he is about to blow up at me, he will laugh silently. His upper lip curls back, and beneath his black wire moustache, his chipmunk teeth look like they're nibbling at a nut. He snorts through his nose. But he never really laughs aloud. He can have his restaurant. I feel sorry for him.

Some nights I can't dispel his rage. One night Roberto, my fellow dishwasher, asks Jean Paul for a raise. Jean Paul starts to shout that he hates this greedy town, he hates the greedy people here, he hates cooking for greedy imbeciles. He hates this restaurant that he owns. He will go back to France and drive a taxi.

"No raise, Roberto!" he screams, pronouncing the name like Robert O. "No raise, Robert O." And he takes a frying pan down from a hook and bangs it over his own head, really whacking himself again and again until blood trickles down his forehead. "See!" he shouts. "See what you all do to me!"

"Okay," Roberto says. "Okay, I guess I don't need the raise. Stop hitting yourself, Jean Paul."

I was about to ask for a raise myself, but I change my mind.

I'm tired but happy when I finish work at two in the morning. Dishwashing isn't the glory job one dreams of, but then again, there's some South American fishermen I read about once who work twenty-two hours a day and suck on raw squid for lunch. And if you're new in town and need a job quick, pearl diving's always there. So I can't complain. It's a great feeling to be through with work, riding in Roberto's truck through the snowy streets, nipping on a beer, heading to Sue Anne's. If it weren't for Sue Anne, I wouldn't be feeling so good, but I enjoy these moments with Roberto before I arrive at her house.

There's a camaraderie between dishwashers, a sense of loyalty to one another. At work, we sound like sentries in the movies. Dragging on a cigarette, Roberto will say a little anxiously, "What do you think they'll hit us with tonight?" And I'll say, "It could get heavy." "We took a real beating last night," he'll say. "We'll be ready for them tonight," I reassure him. "It's the silverware that gets me," he says. "It's quiet so far," I say. He nods. "That's what worries me." We smoke another cigarette and listen for the sound of incoming cutlery.

Some nights when I get to Sue Anne's, she wakes with a tremendous energy. Sits up in bed like there's a burglar in the house. Wants to talk, wants to hear all about my night.

On those nights we bound around her house like the only two people awake in the world. We dance on the pinewood floors. She fixes me bacon and eggs and I eat by candlelight. She shows me her latest photographs. She comes into the bathroom while I shower. I talk to her through the shower curtain, telling her stories about the restaurant, about how I told Jean Paul I'd need a week off to go to the Dishwasher's Convention in Hawaii so I could give my speech on the changing role of the dishwasher in our modern society. After the speech, I'd give a demonstration of my minimalist technique, which does not involve the use of hands, but relies on subtle hip and shoulder movements. She laughs, the most beautiful lavish laugh. When I hear that laugh, I think that nothing can be wrong in the world. I want that laugh to keep ringing out, to grow louder and louder, to float down the street, to wake everyone like a bell. A happy alarm.

In these late hours we talk about what we'll do next month, next year. I think we should go to Peru, I tell her. I've heard there's rivers there where you can pan for gold.

"Pan for gold?" she says.

"You'll like it."

I keep spinning plans, and sometimes she looks up at the ceiling as if she can see a map there. I think of so many places I want to be with her, so many things I want to do with her, and sometimes she looks worried and I have to call to her from far away.

All this winter when she drives off to work in the morning, I get up to scrape the ice from her windshield. She tells me that I shouldn't come out in the cold, that she can scrape her own ice. But it makes me happy to do it.

"I used to scrape Parnelli Jones's windshield in the Indianapolis 500," I tell her.

Freezing, shoes unlaced, stamping my feet in the snow, I await her kiss before she drives away. They are nice kisses and I can't complain. She drives off with courage. Her hands look steady on the wheel, her shoulders solid beneath her coat.

•

But sometimes she doesn't bound up to greet me when I get back from work at two in the morning. When I climb in bed, she only groans and shifts her body to make room for me. On those nights I think she could do without my cold hands and feet, my sour smell, my breath of beer and smoke and onion. I feel like I could keep talking all night, but sometimes she just doesn't have the gas. One night I shake her by the shoulder. "Talk to me."

"Glad you're here," she mumbles, and pats my thigh.

I tell her about the upcoming winner-take-all match with the dishwasher in St. Louis. It's my big chance to be Number One. She's laughing as she falls back asleep. I keep talking anyway, like she can hear me in her dreams. I look out the window, at the ridge of mountains in the moonlight. Even these mountains above our town will change. In a million years, maybe they won't even be there. Everything's changing all the time. Sometimes I feel scared about it all.

Sue Anne tells me she needs a little time to herself to think about things.

"This has sort of been rushing along," she says. "I feel worried, scared, a little confused. You're always making plans for the future, but the plans change all the time. I don't want to get carried away and then get hurt."

"I'm just trying to talk ourselves some place nice," I say.

"I love you, but just give me a little time to become more confident."

She tells me she is going to take a vacation to her hometown, St. Louis, to think about things. She doesn't mention her old boyfriend who lives there.

After work these nights, Roberto parks his truck outside the old rooming house where I live. We drink our beers in the truck because my landlady's a fanatic about noise. Roberto leaves the motor running so we can keep the heater on. The snow falls and encloses us. Roberto talks about finding another job in the spring. "When times are better," he says. I tell him that I may move to India. He says he's tired. I'm tired too. We shake hands. "Good job tonight, buddy," he says. "We took their best shot."

"Good job, partner," I say. "They can't get us down."

I sigh around my room, light candles, dream of Sue Anne. Times will be better in the spring.

I go to the laundromat one day and meet the world's most obnoxious child. He's about two-and-a-half feet high. As I sit reading the newspaper, he keeps running up to me and blowing a noisemaker in my face. "Now you stop that or I'll have to take it away," his mother keeps saying, but she says it in such a vague, washed-out way that it wouldn't stop anybody. The kid takes the noisemaker out of his mouth long enough to stick his tongue out at me.

Nothing's fun any more. One night Jean Paul calls out, "Hey, Number Two dishwasher, dishwasher Ph.D., what technique are you using tonight?"

"The old drowning pearl diver's method," I say, thinking about diving down into one of those big old grimy sinks and not coming up.

Jean Paul comes over and stands beside me at the sink. He puts his arm around me. For a moment I feel like he's my father. For a moment I feel like bawling.

Sue Anne shows up at my door late one night. She's crying. She says she misses me.

"You just want your windshield professionally scraped," I say.

"No, I want to hear you talk," she says. "I want to hear your stories."

"You know what I'd like?" I ask her. "I'd like to get married in a tree."

"Okay," she says. "Let's do it."

"I was thinking maybe we'd live in Samoa for awhile."

"Sure, let's live in Samoa."

"If I can beat that St. Louis dishwasher, we'll have plenty of dough."

Her laughter wakes my landlady, who thunders her stern fists upon my door.

Of late, I use an old, traditional style of washing dishes. The technique was developed in England around 1815, in that fitful time just after the great and terrible War of 1812. Those were hard and lean years, but lovers would join together in hopeful ceremonies, trudging through the snow, carrying their dirty dishes to a peaceful country home. Mingling their dishes in an outdoor sink, they would plunge their hands in and together they would draw forth a plate. Working side by side, they would scrub and polish and hold it aloft, until the plate sparkled in the sun, looking bright and shiny and as precious as a pearl in winter.

Improvising

FOR YEARS I'VE PLAYED A CREEP on the show. I tell the director and writers that I want to become a good guy. Oh come on, they say, you play a convincing creep. Who would believe you've been transformed? Who would like you anyway, if you were transformed? People like a creep. Trying to change your character can only hurt you.

In the show, I've been a pornographer, an adulterer, a backbiter, a blackmailer, a con artist, and an all-around troublesome fellow. I've even done a stint in prison. But I am serious now about reforming.

Well, what do you want? the director asks. Do you want to become a born-again Christian, we could work that in perhaps. No, nothing like that. I want to be good, admirable, loved. But troubled. Questing. The born-agains have all the answers, and I don't want the answers, just the questions. People don't like people with too many answers.

I've been hinting around to Elaine, a former girlfriend, that I may reveal to her husband, Barry, that the child he thinks is his and Elaine's is actually mine and Elaine's. Elaine finally demands, "What do you plan to do?"

"I wish I knew," I say.

"Are you going to tell him?"

I'm supposed to say, "Well, I think we mig ht be able to negotiate something," and give a wicked leer. But instead I say sadly, "What good could come of it?"

Elaine is supposed to say, "You loathsome creature." Instead she only opens her mouth, and her gray, puzzled eyes search my face.

"Fade out," the director shouts. He storms toward us furiously, looks about to explode, and then says, "Hey, that was interesting."

In the show I live alone in a dumpy apartment on the side of town which is supposed to represent corruption and sin. Whenever I tell anyone where I live, they are supposed to arch their eyebrows and say, "Oh. There." When I am introduced to new people, they are supposed to say, "I've heard a lot about you," as if they're wondering if I'm really as rotten as people say.

But now, when people call with shady deals, I turn them down. The writers and the director have cooked up all sorts of schemes for the show, but I've been putting the cork in all of them, which is driving everyone to distraction. Someone will call with a crooked deal, and I'll say, "No. Forget it. Not interested." Then the guy on the other end who has all these other lines to say, will be caught at a loss and mumble something like, "Well, uh, okay, I guess it's off," and hang up.

But the director doesn't know what to do. Since I've had my change of heart our ratings have gone up. People wonder if I'm seriously changing. Some people write in to say they like the change. I was getting boring as a bad guy. Is that it? Am I merely bored with being bad?

What to do, though, about the baby, my son? For awhile I didn't really care. I just wanted to cause trouble for Barry and Elaine. Barry is pretty naive, and seems to lack some basic knowledge of biology. He doesn't get much respect. But he's a nice guy. Sometimes he complains to the director that he wants to be smarter. "Sorry, Barry," the director says. "You were meant to be stupid. You will always be stupid. We need stupid people in this show. Nothing personal."

More and more, I hole up in my room and brood. In the past, in all matters, my motivation was clear, but not my course of action. I wanted to do whatever would cause the greatest amount of trouble, but I did not always know how to achieve that goal. I had to plot and plan and still things might not turn out as I wanted. Now again, my motivation is clear, at least to me. I want to do whatever will cause the greatest good, but I still don't know what course of action to take. So, either way, I'm still in the same fix.

Hm. Trixie, a loose woman, shows up at my shabby little apartment. Trixie only appears when somebody needs to be seduced, but the director doesn't want a long-term relationship to ensue. At one time or another, Trixie has seduced every man on the show. We're a weak lot.

She forces me to lie down on the bed with her, opens my shirt, tickles my navel. "Tell me your deep dark secret about you and Barry and Elaine," she coos.

"What possible good could come of it if you knew?"

"Oh, you're no fun anymore," she says, licking at my ear. "Be a bad boy won't you? Cause trouble for everyone? For the good old days?"

She slides off me, straightens her dress, shakes a finger at me. "You know the problem with you, boy?"

"No." I listen, interested.

"You make everybody feel guilty. You're a louse. Self-righteous. You don't make anyone happy."

"But I just want to be a nice person."

"Well, that's really mean of you." She starts out the door.

"Hey, I still wouldn't mind being seduced. I mean, as long as you're here."

"And selfish." She slams the door behind her. What is one to do?

A distinguished-looking elderly gentleman with a white moustache joins the show. There is some mystery about him. He's always there watching, appearing in doorways.

He meets me in a café one rainy day.

"Who are you, really?" I ask.

"I am your father," he says.

"Well, this is certainly a surprise," I say.

In the past I would have told the old bird to shove off. I'd probably hit him up for a few bucks and put him back on a bus within the hour. Sayonara, Dad, see you in another ten years maybe. I wasn't an emotional sort of guy.

"How come you never came before? Why do you come back now? Where have you been anyway?"

"Those are all certainly questions that deserve answers," he says, standing, picking up his hat. "I'll be back in touch."

Fade out on my puzzled face. The director says, "That was interesting."

"What kind of a stunt are you pulling? My father? That old song and dance?"

"Well, you never had a father," he says. "He had to appear sometime."

"After all these years? Who is he? What does he want from me?"

"We'll see," the director says. "We'll soon see."

Elaine and Barry have gone out for the evening and left me to babysit. This is Elaine's way of letting me see my son. It's the most she ever wants me to have of him. Should I tell the truth to Barry? What good could come of it? Probably none. Perhaps great harm. I don't know. I grow more and more confused the kinder I become.

I haven't reformed completely. Whenever I have a scene with Barry I always borrow five dollars from him. It's my way of getting back at him a little because I can't have my son. "Oh yeah, Barry," I'll say as he's getting ready to leave, "do you think you could spot me five dollars?" Barry's a nice guy and doesn't want to look cheap so he has to shuck over the money, though he's started to wince now when he digs for his wallet. One day he tried to get away with handing me a one. I shrieked like a banshee, held the one up to the camera and cried, "A one! I asked him for a five and he gives me a lousy one!" So the camera zoomed in on the one, and then on to Barry's stricken face. He started whining that it was an honest mistake, and he got so flustered he started shoveling bills at me, until I'd managed to tuck away about twenty bucks. Then he ducked out the door, looking like he'd been caught exposing himself. Then I said, deadpan, to the camera, "There's something about him that I don't like."

Barry doesn't cross me anymore.

The baby cries. I pick him up, rock him. Sleep, child. Our sins are not your sins.

The scene fades as I waltz around the room with my son asleep in my arms.

"Why weren't you there when I needed you?" I ask my father. "There are things I might have told you, confidences we might have shared. I might have turned out differently."

We are in the café again, and it is raining. The director likes to have my father come out of the rain, brush water from his hat and overcoat before sitting. Offstage, just before my father's entrances, someone always zaps him in the face with a squirt gun. I am always struck by the fact that my father is wet.

My father's lips move. He frowns thoughtfully. "Did it ever occur to you that my life has been so out of control that it is amazing, even now, to find myself here, speaking to you?"

"Well, that explains everything."

"No one gets to choose his father. You happened to get me." The old man picks up his hat, looks at me. "I am here now. That is what matters perhaps. Yes? I am your father. We have a chance now. To be together. To make a life for ourselves."

"I don't need a father now," I snap. "Not after all this time."

He puts on his hat and goes off into the rain, a sad, wet-looking, distinguished elderly gentleman. I run to the door and shout, "Father!" The scene fades with me standing at the doorway, doubled over with pain.

"Perfecto," the director cries.

Elaine and Barry have gone out again and I am alone with my son. He sleeps in his cradle and I speak to him. "I wish that you could tell me what to do. Is the best thing for me to disappear from your life? I don't know what happened. We are sons without fathers, fathers without sons. What if I showed up thirty years from now and asked to be taken in? Would you believe me if I said that I'd had no control? I'm afraid the truth can only hurt you. You will never know me as your father."

"Cut," the director shouts. "You were supposed to say, 'One day you'll be mine no matter what I have to do.' "

"I can't say that line."

"Well, you're going to be in big trouble now. Big trouble. Wait and see."

But the ratings are still going up. He can't fire me. I am the show.

It's raining. We are in the café. My father's face is dripping wet again. I have an urge to wipe it off with my handkerchief.

"I'm glad you've come back," I say. "That's all. Whatever has happened before doesn't matter now. I want you as my father. I want you to move in with me."

"Yes, well." He looks at his coffee. "There is only one small problem."

"What, father? Don't tell me that you're going away. Please don't tell me that."

"No, it's not that."

"What is it then?"

"It's the small matter of my hotel bill. I'm a little, shall we say, short?"

"I see, uh, how much do you need?"

"I think about a hundred and fifty dollars would cover it nicely."

"I see. Well, anything for you, Pops." I take out my checkbook.

"Of course, it would be nice to have just a little something left over."

"Mmhm."

After my father leaves, I notice that his coffee cup and spoon are missing. The camera pans to my face. "Jesus Christ," I say, "my old man's a kleptomaniac."

Besides being a kleptomaniac, it turns out my father has a bad habit of getting lost. The police are always bringing him home. The thing is, my father doesn't much care where he is. He'll wander around a shopping mall all day, or stand in the parking lot at St. Edward's Boys' School.

He's eating me out of house and home. For a thin old man, he can sure pack it away. The sight of him devouring five sunnyside eggs every morning, as he carefully pats his moustache after every bite, somehow unnerves me.

Now and then I throw a tantrum. I rave at him for not being around all these years. He'll only look at the ceiling and say something like, "It's amazing really, to think one is even here at all, to discover one is anything more than an atom, a minute floating particle." Well, what can one say to that?

He sleeps on the couch in his clothes. When you have been a vagrant for sixty years, he explains, you are always ready to leave.

I know the director is trying to drive me crazy, but it's not working. I'm getting closer to the old man, getting used to his ways.

About my own son, I have done nothing. Sometimes I think it would be best to tell the truth, sometimes I think the truth would ruin everyone. What to do? I lose weight. I begin to bite my nails. I forget to bum money from Barry.

The only solace in my life, curiously enough, is my father, eating his eggs, getting yolk in the corner of his moustache, sleeping in his clothes, stealing coffee cups and spoons.

One day my father arranges to meet me in the café. It is raining. I hand my father a handkerchief to wipe off his face.

"Bad news," he says.

"What is it?"

"I would like to tell you that I am proud to have you as my son, that I will never go away, that you and I will grow closer and closer."

"That sounds swell, Pops."

"Yes, I would like to tell you those things. But you see, it turns out that I'm not your father after all. I am an imposter." He puts on his hat and gets up from the table. He pauses in the doorway. "I am sorry. It would have been nice. Don't call me Pops anymore." He goes off into the rain, another coffee cup, a spoon, and my handkerchief in his coat pocket.

I turn to the director. "No. Oh no. Don't do this."

"Fade," the director shouts. "Perfect. He's destroyed. No father, no son. Nada. You asked for it, sonny boy."

Soft Song of the Sometimes Sane

MR. NORMALITY AM I. Play a pretty fair game of golf. My drives are long and straight, my putting sound. I can't hit a nine iron worth a crap though. From about a hundred yards in, my game stinks.

The real problem is that I lack a clear sense of purpose. Along about the eighth hole, I wonder what on earth I am doing out here on this long, hilly, windswept, sandtrap-strewn course. On these cool, dying autumn evenings, as the light pales and fades to a heartbreak whitish-gray, I am filled with despair. Who are these other golfers I am partnered with? I am never paired with wise, grizzled old-timers who reveal great secrets of life and love. I am partnered with farters, manic-depressives, and unemployed tax accountants. By the time I sink my last putt on the ninth hole, I loathe them and they loathe me.

Family Background

For years I've been trying to prove that I can safely drink again. Even after they sent me to the hospital ten years ago, I still wasn't convinced. I come from a drinking family. We had beer for breakfast. My father was a lawyer, but he's retired now. He whistles when he drinks. He gets red in the face and increasingly friendly. People find my mother charming, and justifiably so. When my parents visited me at the rehab, the social worker was disgusted with me.

"Such nice parents," he said. "What the hell happened to you?" It was just my luck to get a cranky social worker. Social workers are not all the nice guys they're made out to be.

Up to Old Tricks

Lately when I speak to strangers, I fake a British accent. I don't know why. Maybe I think it will protect me somehow. When I was a teenager I would go to parties, and after several beers I would speak with a British accent. I thought it would make me appear unique, but after a while some of the bigger guys would hold me under the beer keg and put the spigot in my mouth until I bloated. I was known as a character. I'd memorized a few lines of Shakespeare and most of my friends, who couldn't read or write very well, thought I was a mad genius. But this still did not prevent them from holding me under the keg and forcing beer down my throat. But they could not really harm me because I was not one of them. I was British. I was a British spy. I had cyanide in my shoes.

Evasive Tactics

Walking through downtown Berkeley, I'm afraid that I may be mugged. There's a lot of lunatics on the street and they all want my money. Lunatics aren't all the nice guys they're sometimes made out to be. So I go down the street, whirling, changing direction, crossing to the other side, dodging cars, praising the Lord. Keeping the lunatics confused, you see. Listen. Downtown Berkeley is full of lunatics. Go to Boise.

Teeth

My teeth are going bad. Even after I've brushed them, they've got a sticky, gummy feeling. I was in New Orleans once, sitting on a bus. Across the aisle sat a lunatic. They come at me like flies. He was a great conversationalist. Told me this: "I put four holes in Jesus. Downtown Waco. I shot Jesus. Put four holes in him. He got back up. He was the real Jesus."

And you, sir, are a real, true, certified loon.

My friend, the lunatic, sneered out the bus window at some loitering vagrant types. "Trash," he said. "Just trash. I, for one, have never neglected to brush my teeth."

Not only was he a lunatic, but like many lunatics, he was an intolerant son-of-a-bitch.

I, too, have never neglected to brush my teeth. But will that save them? Will it save me?

Professional Life

I am the Director of Humanities at a small college. It is a good title and the pay is not bad. I don't actually do much of anything. We are a bottom-of-the-barrel school. We are on probation. Our students are almost all foreigners and those who aren't are Americans who couldn't get into a decent school. I'm a crappy teacher and an even crappier administrator. I tell jokes to my English class for half an hour every day and let them out early. I give them all A's. They love me.

As a director, I don't know who or what I am supposed to direct. I lack a clear sense of purpose. I sit in my office and drink coffee and read the newspaper. Sometimes I bang on the typewriter, really get the keys clacking so that people will hear the machine and think I am busy. I take three-hour lunches, telling the Dean I am out recruiting new students. As far as I can tell, everyone is very happy with the way I am doing my job.

Home Life

My wife is a beautiful, kind woman who watched me go mad once before, ten years ago. They called it alcoholism, but after they dried me out, they discovered I was still crazy. This was in the waning days of electro-shock, but they gave me a few jolts anyway. I was one of their last customers. It didn't help my mind much, but for some reason it increased my sex drive. I left the hospital a better lover, for which my wife, at any rate, was grateful.

I am not happy. I've been telling my wife this lately. What she wants to know is why. I find this astonishingly simple of her and yet astonishingly difficult to answer. Why? Why? Why? I groan at the question as if it is incredibly stupid, which, of course, hurts her feelings. But the truth is I can't answer.

I have no right to be unhappy. Why am I going mad again? In

my case, it is only a lack of character. That is all. I am the fellow on the bus who plugged Jesus. I am willful. I am the worst lunatic of all. I deserve no sympathy. You should kick me in the ass.

Why?

Because I lack a clear sense of purpose. I feel apart from God. I feel apart from my fellow man. I feel apart from my wife. I feel apart from myself. I intensely dislike our cat.

Retracing My Steps

I'm going home. Back home. Down south. Kiss the wife. Honey, I've got to go visit the folks, see what's up.

I take a few days off from work and fly home. Momma's drinking. Daddy's drinking. Brothers are drinking. We barbecue a bunch of beef and drink. Daddy whistles. Momma keeps hugging me, glad I'm home. Brothers and I practice chip shots in the backyard The old castrated beagle retrieves the balls, carries a ball around in his mouth, showing off—look, I still got balls. You a good ole hound dog, you is. I shank a nine iron and break the kitchen window. Daddy yells. But we're all happy as hell.

So happy I can't figure it. Can't walk, can't talk, start to cry, vomit all over myself.

Check-in Time

Dry me out time. Hello, Mr. Psychiatrist.

Nothing? Nothing ever troubled you? Nothing bad ever happened to you?

Well, I was fondled.

He is delighted to hear this.

But frankly it wasn't all that bad. Was twelve. Spent the night at a friend's. We slept in the living room on the floor. Woke up and his old man was lying next to me. Had his arm around me. I thought he'd made a mistake, was walking in his sleep or something and just happened to lie down next to me. Just happened to have his hand on my little, twelve-year-old pencil. I was embarrassed for him. I knew he'd be embarrassed when he woke up. His face was scratchy against mine. His hand felt kind of gnarly. I moved a little, pretended I was just waking. His hand tightened a little. My fellow was trapped. His breathing was hot in my ear. Didn't move. Didn't say anything. Thought he'd be mad at me if he woke up. He had his nose in my ear. In the morning I didn't say anything. He didn't say anything. I didn't think he remembered. I wasn't sure it had happened. I started taking a lot of showers. I could feel that hand there. Made me wince. That feeling like when chalk screeks across the blackboard. Hey, let go of that! I'd practice shouting. Hey you, let go there, hands off! Next time I came over, Leroy saying, hey Dad, can he stay over? Can Jimmy stay over? Why sure, Jimmy can stay over. Oh no, no sir, I gotta go. Oh no, sure, we'd be happy to have Jimmy, I'll call his mom. Oh, she won't let me, I just know she won't let me. Oh, I'm sure she will, I'll just give her a call. And I'm dying, I'm shaking, but I'm trapped, I'm on the floor, up all night, watching, waiting, and he doesn't come and I think, I did, I did, I imagined it all. And it all fades away and I forget and like his old man again, he's always taking us out for hamburgers and he lets us have a beer sometimes, so when he asks me to go fishing with them I say sure, cause I really do want to go fishing. And we're in the camper getting undressed for bed, and there's two beds and Leroy says, I want my own bed, you can sleep with my old man. Now, wait a minute here, thinks I, and his old man's drooping his arm around me and leading me to bed.

It happened again?

I had a fever in the morning. I hardly remembered.

So you felt powerless?

Powerless. Sure. I felt powerless.

Well, I don't know how much all this has to do with my problems, but it makes my shrink happy anyway.

Release

Check-out time. Kiss the wife. I was fondled as a child, I tell her. I'm recovering. Slowly. Be kind.

Bundle of energy. Sober. Wide awake. Dynamic lectures at school. Foreign students impressed. Throw roses at me every class. Wave flags. God bless America.

Oh, and I am so very tolerant to the man who asks for money. I am open. I do not try to protect myself. Here, sir, is a quarter.

Here, sir, is a dollar. Here, sir, is my billfold. I, too, was once a lunatic. I was fondled, you see. What's that? You put four holes in Jesus? Well, I'm sure He won't hold it against you, but for heaven's sake don't let it happen again.

Purpose

Getting cool, that old sun going down earlier and earlier. They're going to shut down the course tomorrow. Last day of the season, I shoot a forty-three. Great score for me. Jazzed up now. Decide to play the back nine. All by myself. Partner slumps away to the parking lot, had enough. Thank goodness. Was playing with a troubled taxidermist. Worried, you know. "Taxidermy business is going to the dogs. It's those goddamn vegetarians." Kept scratching at the crotch of his polyester pants, lime-green, just before each shot. Disturbed me somehow.

I lose four balls on the thirteenth. One after another, chip them into the water hazard. Wide, wide, wide water hazard, stinky, muddy, a bog, foul bog, devourer of balls and men, hopes perish here. Step up to the brink and heave my clubs in after the balls. There they go, down, down, into the bog, beneath the muddy water.

I turn to leave. A sudden pain in the chest. A heart attack. No, a sudden realization. I love golf. I love the great game of golf. I want to come back next season. And the season after that, as I grow wobbly, led about, half-blind, I'll totter to my ball, take aim, ah, I must look upon those red flags that flutter in the wind, take aim, take aim again.

I suddenly have a clear sense of purpose. I must save my clubs! I will regain my clubs. I will practice my chip shots. I will improve my game. I will not despair. I will be back next season!

I wade in after my clubs. Water's deeper than I think. I'm up to my chest. Water rat dives out of the bushes. My shoes squish around in the mud. I kick around through the weeds, trying to feel the clubs.

The groundsman drives up on a cart and looks at me. Not quite a frown. There is a touch of stern kindness on his leathery face. He is dressed all in khaki and wears a pith helmet, to protect his noggin from errant balls. Sitting in his cart, he looks like a general. Or he is a sad old psychiatrist of the fairways. He knows what strange torments we suffer as we batter our way from tee to hole. He has witnessed it all. He has seen the farters play, the manic-depressives, the unemployed tax accountants, the troubled taxidermists, has seen us all pass, all blow our shots, hit into traps, lose our balls in the hazard, bounce off trees, throw our clubs, break our clubs, swear, shout, dance, holler, and all, all out of love.

"I've lost my clubs," I tell him. "I hit four balls into the water and then I lost my temper and I threw my bag in after the balls. Now I want my clubs back."

He only stares at me.

I try a different approach. I laugh. I say, "I'm sure I've got a shot if I can find my ball."

He nods his head, ever so slightly, and climbs out of his cart. He steps to the bank and, with a sigh, rolls up the bottoms of his trousers.

The Things I
Don't Know About

ERNEST HEMINGWAY ONCE SAID that when he was a young writer he decided to write one story about everything he knew something about. When I was in my mid-twenties, setting out to be a writer, I was panicky about all the things I did not know about.

For one thing, I knew nothing about guns. My readings of contemporary fiction had made me pretty well certain that no book, and certainly no book by a native Texan, could climb to fame without at least the appearance of a gun, and preferably a veritable profusion of guns, liberally used. I would need to write lines like: Wilson coolly sighted his .430xx2 semi-loaded Swiss Mitzer three degrees north, allowing for the torque of the heavy-oxide, brass-rimmed bullet....

But even as I brooded over guns, something else I didn't understand, or didn't want to understand, grasped my attention. Now that I was living briefly at home again, after returning from Mexico where I'd been writing a bad book and teaching English to support myself, I became aware of my mother's coughing. Her wet phlegmy hacking. Her wheezing. Her throat clearing. Her spitting into a handkerchief. Her struggles to breathe.

Shortly after my return, she'd taken me aside. "There's something I need to tell you" she said, outside the hearing of my younger brothers. "Now, I don't want you to worry, but I've been told I have a touch of emphysema." As I stared at her, she gave a girlish laugh, her eyes still lively then, full of light. She nudged my shoulder. "Now don't worry. It's just a touch." A touch of emphysema? Like a touch of cancer? A touch of AIDS?

But she didn't slow down much—worked as a secretary, kept up the housework, did her typing and research in the evenings, attended a college class or two. The emphysema had years left to do its work, years left before it stole away her happiness and hope and finally her life. In fact, there was only one thing it did not steal. In her last months, as she lay in bed, wasted to the bone, her eyes frightened and hollow beneath the oxygen mask, she held to love, to her capacity to love, as tightly as her skeletal, papery fingers clutched her rosary beads and our hands. That was her final fight; she battled not for time, but for love.

During the day, she managed, to some degree, to conceal and stifle the cough. But she went to bed earlier than the rest of us, and then the coughing set in in full force. It followed a predictable pattern. First a few, rather mild, clearings of the throat. Then an uneasy silence. Then a cough from deeper in the chest, and another, increasing in tempo until the coughs came one on top of another, formed an unbroken chain, and then finally a wet throat-clearing release. An expectant silence. Then the cycle was repeated, but by this time the coughing had turned fierce so that as the pattern reached its crescendo I thought her chest must be torn apart, and indeed as time went on, her coughing sometimes broke a brittle bone.

Perhaps, I hoped, there was a remedy for one of my failings. I turned to my seventeen-year-old youngest brother, George. George knew guns; he was something of a collector and the only one of my five siblings who hunted. I was embarrassed to tell him why I wanted to know about guns; I just told him I wanted to accompany him to the shooting range.

He was delighted at the possibility of an ally. Guns had been a sore spot in our family since the year before when George brought home his first rack of horns. My father remarked that he saw no sport in killing a defenseless creature, and my mother, ever vigilant toward the hazards posed by animal parasites, sprayed copious quantities of Lysol on the horns and skullcap. For several weeks, my vegetarian brother Sean, a year older than George, feigned fits of horror whenever he beheld the horns mounted on George's bedroom wall. As George read in bed, Sean appeared in the doorway, with a quaking finger pointed at the horns as if at Banquo's ghost, clutched his throat and popped his eyes wide, wailing, "Why? Why did he die?" As George ignored him, he swooned and thrashed about on the floor, blubbering, "Why! Oh why! Oh noble forest creature! May God forgive my brother!" George sighed, muttered, "Asshole," and hid his eyes behind his book.

For the last few days, ever since his girlfriend had broken up with him and the crown on his front tooth had snapped off yet again, George had been bearing himself with a certain fatalistic, slump-shouldered, Devil's Island stoicism. But his steps were jaunty as he carried his leather case to the shooting stand. He gave me a snaggle-toothed pirate's grin and produced his pride and joy, a gun he'd assembled in secrecy, fearing that once again the family would fail to appreciate his endeavors. He ran his hand lovingly over the smooth wooden stock of the old-fashioned Daniel Boone-style powder rifle, and as I stared at the flintlock it slowly sank in on me that I was doomed. While the other writers got rich and famous arming their heroes with high-tech weaponry, my good guys would be reduced to abject, absurd missions of doom. They'd fire off one futile round and spend the rest of their time pathetically scampering for a safe place to cram down the ramrod. What self-respecting hero would arm himself with a one-shot muzzle-loaded powder rifle? I'd have to create louts, eccentrics, misfits, incompetents. The hell with suspense; I'd have to write satire.

But I clucked with appropriate enthusiasm over the rifle. Westerns? Maybe I could write westerns? But I did not know much about horses, and I sensed that could be a drawback.

Fire leapt from the muzzle. Smoke wreathed our heads and filled our nostrils. My shoulder ached from the fierce buck of the gun. My ears rang, became deaf to any sound but the explosion of the gun. George and I grinned and gesticulated at each other. We'd attracted a crowd of admirers. I remember the sheer happiness on George's face, his eyes wet from the smoke, his snaggle-toothed grin saying things like: Isn't it beautiful? Haven't I made something lovely and fine? He was gentle with me, his older brother, pouring the powder in for me, loading the shot, working the ramrod. I was caught up in the moment with him; we were side by side at the Alamo, at Gettysburg, two against a thousand, shoulder to shoulder, man to man, brother to brother. Over and over the gun belched forth its fire, and though quite a few years have passed now, I think of that day when I think of George. He was magnificent, his head wreathed in smoke, his cheeks splashed with tears, firing away on that crisp golden autumn afternoon as if each explosion might hold at bay some coming sorrow, might overcome the other sound that had disturbed our suburban slumbers.

When the coughing started up at night, Sean and George and I would gather in George's room, the room at the far end of the hallway of our ranch-style house. It was something unspoken between us. We just needed to gather, to sit with one another as the cough travelled down the long hallway. Two of us sat on the edge of the bed and the other took up the desk chair. We'd hear our father checking on her. We talked of many things, laughed at times, but we'd catch ourselves clenching our hands, gritting our teeth against the sound of the cough. Every few nights, as if I'd forgotten, I'd ask my brothers, "How long has she been like this?" And they would glance at each other as if they too had forgotten, as if each hoped the other might recall. Then finally one would say, "Oh. A while now." And the other would nod and say, "Yeah. It's been a while."

I went away again. I went away for a while. And each time I came back, I'd find she'd grown a bit worse, but she lived long enough to see me married, lived long enough to fall in love with my young children and to have them love her.

After my mother's funeral, Sean and George and I gathered, as of old, in George's old bedroom. We were laughing and crying over our memory of mother coming in to apply Lysol to the horns which were still mounted on the wall. Tears ran down George's face. His front crown had snagged off just that morning over a hard piece of candy; caught between tears and laughter, he looked as he had on the day fifteen years before at the rifle range. He is my younger brother by almost a decade, but at times he seems older. I have kept my hair and he has lost much of his, though he combs long strands over from the side to cover the balding patch on top. I have maintained my weight, but he has grown heavier. He's become something of a tycoon in real estate and oil, and I think his business affairs and his troubled love life have burdened him, put a weight upon his shoulders. He deals with things I do not know about.

When I lived back at home that year, my mother was researching our roots. She'd become a skillful researcher and she could write well herself, but she wanted me to put our roots into fictional form. She was particularly enamored with the story of her great-grandmother Rebecca, whose husband had died when she was young, leaving her alone with her children on a ranch in hostile Comanche territory just north of San Antonio.

I could embellish, she said, make it interesting, add some action.

My mother had always encouraged my fiction, so indeed I did embellish. Apparently, there had been a few times when Indians had run off with the horses or where outlaws had camped on the land. Rebecca kept a shotgun handy, but there was no record of her using it except against an occasional rattlesnake or to scare off a coyote.

But perhaps my recent curiosity about guns flavored my writing. I turned my great-great-grandmother Rebecca into a killing machine. Nightly, droves of Comanches attacked the ranch and Rebecca blew them away, firing out the window as they whirled their horses in exultant rings around the cabin. The high casualty rate of the Comanches diminished their esprit de corps not in the slightest; the next night they'd swoop in again. The nightly sieges became such old hat to the children that they slept right through the gunfire, and when Rebecca got bored with the action, she'd fling upon the cabin door and fire off a few one-handed salvos as she hitched her skirts and chased the Indians across the moonlit prairie.

Then I created a madman named Buck, who was sinister and degenerate enough to frighten away even the stalwart Comanches. He terrorized Rebecca and the children. In the night he'd slaughter a horse, then build a small campfire just out of gun range and in the eerie light of the fire he'd perform disgusting rituals. He'd eat the horse's liver raw, smear his chest with blood, drop his trousers and moon the terrified, mesmerized pioneers in the cabin. He moved his campfires closer each night, crept around the cabin at all hours, walked on the roof, made belching noises outside the windows. There was, in the story, some hint of sexual urgency, even a mild flavor of misguided romance.

One night as Buck danced before the fire, Rebecca stole out carrying the trusty shotgun. As she crossed the field, the fire suddenly went out. She was alone, beneath the moonlight. Her heart raced. Where was Buck? She listened. She turned to run back to the cabin. Then he was upon her. He threw her to the ground, knelt on her, pinned her, his horrid horse liver breath in her face. He hoisted high a great knife, freeing one of Rebecca's hands. It was his fatal mistake. With the derringer hidden up her sleeve, Rebecca fired one cool, almost silent, round into his heart. He jumped back, as if snakebit, then rolled over on his back on the prairie grass. He lay looking up at the stars in some vast final wonderment. Smiled faintly. Then expired.

Mother chuckled a couple of times when she read the story, but overall she was not pleased.

"I said you could embellish, but did you have to make it so silly? Now I want you to write the real story."

"Okay. Okay. I'm sorry," I said.

So I wrote it again. I kept it straightforward. The shotgun was relegated to a minor role.

This time she said, "It seems kind of flat."

Critics! Editors! My own mother!

I gave up; I avoided the project. The years went on and mother kept compiling our roots. Near the end she became obsessed with getting it all down.

She called one day to ask for my help. She wasn't counting on me for too much, she said. She'd farmed out a lot of the project to my brothers and sisters. I could just do the part about her great grandmother Rebecca. I'd always had a flair for her character, she thought, a kind of affinity. I could embellish. A bit.

I brought the shotgun back into use. A few Indians and outlaws menaced the ranch, but I was more subdued about the bloodshed. Buck made a reappearance as a travelling whiskey trader with a certain glinty-eyed, leering expression. I depicted life on the range as accurately as one who does not know much about it can. With trepidation, I mailed the story off to my mother. A few days later she called me. She sounded happy. As happy as she could sound with her labored breathing. She liked it, she said. She liked it very much.

"There's another story about our roots that I'm going to work on, Mom," I said. "I want you to read it when I'm through."

She paused. "How long will it take?"

But I was busy with work and with the kids and the call from my father came sooner than I'd expected. She was back in the hospital. I needn't come home yet, he said. He didn't think it was too bad. Then it got worse. Then it got better. We thought. There was an operation the doctors could do. They could remove a blood clot from her lungs. You don't need to come home, my father said, it's not so bad yet. And my mother from her hospital bed got on the phone and wheezily echoed him. "Don't come home. You're need-ed there." Then she paused, gathered her strength. "I love you. I love all of you."

She was too weak. She did not live through the operation.

And I was not there.

In the other story I wanted to write, I would have told of my mother marrying my father when she was seventeen. I would have told of her working at the drugstore and at her parents' small boarding house when my father, nineteen, went off to war. I would have told of her raising six children and of the sorrow (what I could imagine of it) of losing one to an institution. I would have written of small things; of an evening while my father was still away at work, when she might look up from the pinto beans she was cooking, cast a long gaze at a darkening sky and pronounce, "It looks like a blue norther," saying it in such a way that set it as far apart from a regular old norther as night is from day. We children marvelled at the forces of wind and rain descending upon us. We huddled deliciously close. The beans, flavored by ham bone, simmered on. Mother was near; our house would not buckle.

Last year, after my mother died, my oldest son, four then, re-marked, "Grandma got extinct. Like the dinosaurs." But rather than missing her less, he seems to miss her more, or perhaps it is only the idea of Grandma he misses.

More and more, he asks me why his grandmother died and what he is really asking is: Why does anyone die? And his heart is heavy at times with a new fear—that I too will die and abandon him. And there is even a darker fear, one which he can't articulate yet, one which he doesn't want to articulate.

He remembers his grandmother's struggles to breathe, and he knows something about that himself. He's been too many times to the far edge of an asthmatic attack, been rushed to the hospital in the night, injected with epinephrine. And during the milder attacks I've walked him in the night, singing to him, gentling him into my shoulder, whispering to him the names of the stars, the few I know, and when I am quiet he nudges me and says: Show me the stars again, Daddy, show me the stars, and I make up names for the ones I don't know. We walk on through the night, gazing in wonder at the stars, the dogs next door going berserk on the other side of our rickety cedar fence.

He usually asks his questions when we are driving in the car, just the two of us. I try not to avoid the subject, but then again I'm only too willing to hustle us off to a T-ball game or a swimming or soccer practice. I cheer him on, whacking my palms together, trying to lose myself in the resounding clap of hands.

But riding home he returns to the question, and it is worse now because it is twilight and the autumn is deepening, the days grow-ing short. The tires hum on the road and the lights turn on in the houses, and as I drone on and on, trying to explain about life and death, the nature of time passing, he looks at me and I realize I sound, more and more, like I don't know what I am talking about.

Robert Garner McBrearty was raised in San Antonio, Texas, and now lives in Colorado, where he teaches fiction writing at the University of Colorado. A graduate of the Iowa Writers' Workshop, he has received many awards for his fiction, including a Pushcart Prize and fellowships to the Macdowell Colony and the Fine Arts Work Center in Provincetown, Massachusetts. McBrearty's stories have been published in numerous literary quarterlies, including *Missouri Review, Mississippi Review, New England Review,* and *Confrontation.* **A Night at the Y** is his first published collection.